Cry

WaterColors

d2-Edition

Cry

WaterColors

d2-Edition

by

Carlos Alvarado

Determined2 Publishing

Requests for permission to make copies of any part of this work should be mailed to:

Permissions Department
Determined2 Publishing
PO Box 361, Lantana, FL 33465

ISBN: 978-0-9995671-2-8

Printed in the United States of America for Determined2 Publishing Library of Congress

Control Number:

Acknowledgment

Taking a look back can often propel you forward;
that was my intent for undertaking

Cry Watercolors: d2 Edition.

When I first began to write, it was to fulfill an innate desire; but when the characters began to assume a personality, I wanted to share them with anyone willing to read what I wrote: my goal became getting published.

Independent writers take a big gamble in search of a
market for their art. That you have opened my book
and given it a look is what I worked for,
and I am most grateful.

It is with my sincerest gratitude
that I dedicate this book to
all of you wanting to read what I have written,
even when I'm deeply shadowed
by those in the limelight.

Prologue

From on top of his daddy's lap, Mark gripped the steering wheel and stretched to see over the dashboard. Swerving wildly, he tried to maneuver the car along the road. His father's hands, spread open like butterfly wings, gently eased his impetuous turns.

The veins that coursed the back of the hands that guided him seemed as thick as the shoelace he had learned to knot earlier in the day. Mark loosened his hold on the wheel and compared the length of his fingers to those of his father's. There was nowhere he'd rather be than on the lap of the strongest man in all the world.

Mark shifted his weight and looked up to his father's face and returned the smile that greeted him. Glancing back to just above the dashboard, he imagined himself driving the car down the road.

◆◆◆

In recollection, it was not the sun that shone on their Sunday's drive around the park that Mark treasured, nor the wind he felt that whished through the branches of the willow trees, nor the animal-clouds he counted while laying on prickly blades of grass. What he cherished most was the memory of his father's smile, and of a world in which he could never be hurt.

If it could always have been Sunday, Mark thought before he slept, so many years later.

◆ ◆ ◆

It was not Sunday, and he had long since learned to steer a car in a straight course, but there remained phantoms that haunted him in sleep.

Cloistered in the darkness of the bedroom, his sleep faltered in dreams that yielded to troubled memories; and these were of family he rarely thought about, friends he had long ago lost track of, and characters created for the stories he wrote but were now his sole companions. In a distortion created by a childhood guilt, all these images glared at him as if in judgment. Intending for a conciliation, he pieced together their accusations.

The dreams told of a distant place and another time, a past that seemed to belong to someone else; but among the images, he recognized himself—the cloaked character that gripped his lapels against a cold no one else felt.

Saintly icons, robed in mourning purple, buttressed a church. Worshippers, bent on their knees, prayed in repentance for sins their sufferings had revealed. Self-deprecating penances, dispensed in the isolation of the confessional, guided their psalms. He was cloaked in the purple shroud of Catholic Lent.

Mark had grown up in the implacable culture of Hispanic Catholicism, where sorrow, guilt, and prayer formed the cornerstones for primal-absolution. Through this spiritual purification, one gained God's regard for the dispensation from judgment and granting of rewards.

The rituals of the Catholic universe in the early 1960s

offered comfort for the world in which he lived. Were it not for his imagination, this solace might have been his as well; but fairy tales can displace a child's life.

As real as himself, the angels, stewards of the holy Catholic doctrine, stood in judgment of his every thought and act. Mark feared never doing right, and he found no hiding place. At night, while his family slept peacefully, he was often tormented with vivid imaginings of godly disapproval of his daily acts. Crueler than the slap of his parents' hands was the emptiness he felt in his nightly lament. It churned in his gut and trembled with cold to the sphincter of his anus. This nightly world, suctioned into the hollow of his chest, was the loneliness he feared eternity to be.

At seven, supposedly too young to experience desperation, Mark challenged his confusion. In the silence of his darkened room, he firmly held the point of a knife against his belly. From the pit it made pressed against his flesh, he felt the warm trickle of blood. Pain turned to anger when he realized it was on the promise of eternal reward that God held sway over his life. Without eternity, he reasoned, there would be no need for judgment. Thus his recurrent agony would be resolved. The knife fell to the floor when he asked God that he be forgiven an eternal existence.

A divine response was delivered that morning by an angel in a police uniform. The messenger's dark skin contrasted with the bitter cold of the message given his mother at the front door. Her piercing cry was a siren announcing his father's death in a car accident.

Death had never been as real as eternity, but the silence of his home and the sorrow of his mother told that one was the same as the other. As she cried quietly in her room, Mark watched from afar. He felt her pain the loneliness of his tormented nights. It was God's punishment for the sacrilege of his petition.

On the cemetery lawn was dug a dark, rectangular hole.
Mark looked away to the black polish of his new stiff shoes.
Brown dirt thumped upon the lid of his father's coffin.
His heels hurt where the shoes rubbed.

Priestly incense sifted through the smoggy air.
The dirt would feel good if only his feet were bare.
His mother's cry pealed like an offering bell,
And only he knew why his father had died.

When a mound covered the coffin, his mother embraced him into his older brother and sister. Their tears were salty on his lips, but his face remained dry. He tripped on the stiff shoes and fell away from their caresses. Into the dirt he dug his fingers and screamed in silent prayer. He feared they would know it had been his fault.

Silence extended beyond his prayers, and he retreated into his imagination. In that world, characters harbored thoughts and aspirations he feared for himself. Mark became isolated amidst a family that sheltered him with love.

◆ ◆ ◆

It was Christmas Eve, Midnight Mass, and Mark was twenty-two years old. Incense filled the hollow of the church. Prayers were sung in solemn tones. Bells chimed like shattered crystals. His heel ached where it rubbed against the leather of his shoe. He had loved his father, but had hoped for the dispensation of his guilt—there was none in the penance of the confessional, nor the graces of Communion. But the cool marble felt good below his bare feet when he walked out of the church.

In place of the rigid order of his Catholicism, he fell into the turmoil of self-doubt. He filled conversations with empty sentences so as not to reveal his lack of social graces; and laughed at jokes that were not funny to conceal his own witless humor. In pretending to reciprocate love, he hoped to deflect his inadequacy to receive it. It was only onto the words he wrote that he could entrust his passion.

That summer, Mark graduated from the University of California in Los Angeles with a degree in Literature. No job prospects were handed him with the diploma, so he set out on an introspective trek through the western states. In the abandoned mining towns along the mountain ranges of California and Nevada, he found his muse.

The crackling of dry gravel below his booted feet was the only sound on the hill above the ghost town of Hamilton, Nevada. Except for the warm breeze, everything in the cemetery remained still, as befitted a place of the dead. A single wooden marker drew his attention. Its weathered inscription read, "Mark—1873—Age 22."

Mustard-colored sage covered the flat burial site as if the ground had never been dug. Motionless, he stood to the side of the grave and stared as if at the entombed within. His imagination wandered to the encircling barren hills that appeared as an empty canvas upon which to paint a life worthier than his own. He colored in the adventure he had only read about and, from the torrid air he breathed, Mark imagined a carnal passion he had only hoped for.

Time passed across his shadow. Were it not for the

strengthening of the wind, he would have stood as still as a corpse. The breeze stirred him from reflection to read the epitaph once more; it was his own essential truth: *dead at the age of twenty-two.*

◆◆◆

As if motivated by envy of the adventures and passion he infused his characters with, Mark decided to legitimize his imagination through professional writing. As a book reviewer for a regional entertainment magazine, he chronicled the talents of other writers. At the age of thirty-three, frustrated with the lack of his creativity, he accepted a position as a columnist for *Western Ways* magazine in San Jose.

The need to move out of Los Angeles was never questioned by those that knew him; after all, a journalistic position was rare in the esoteric field of his fascination—ghost towns of the Old West.

Wanting to rid himself of reminders of an encumbered past, he whittled down his belonging to fit into the trunk of his car. With the prospect of a new beginning, he surged north on US 101. But once settled in San Jose, all that changed was his detachment. As family and friends tired of telephone and greeting card communication, Mark withdrew to the company of the characters in his tales.

Complacency in his solitude gave him an emotional balance that allowed him success in his writing. He would have been content—were it not for the desires of the flesh.

Susan had been his last romance—whose love he had accepted conditionally. Their relationship became a test of wills, in which his inevitably was abdicated. Without a will, he felt no drive, and so their relationship languished. The separation was formalized by an indictment of his lack of backbone. Her charge remained uncontested when she walked away.

That was three years ago, and the pattern of his solitude had been re-established. With it came freedom from judgment, the cruelest of which had been his own. He became the lonely man that everyone considered a pariah, which no one knew how to react to but his friend Spencer Tate, who simply thought it was *sad*.

Middle age had come upon him as predictably as desert weeds tumble on a storm. Recently inflicted by a flurry of recurrent chills, which he attributed to physical changes of aging, Mark awaited an appointment with his doctor.

◆ ◆ ◆

In his dreams was revealed a life without anticipation, but was free of remorse. In his life, vulnerability was a theme, but not a resource for adventure. He controlled his world through imagination, and the keys of his laptop were its toggles.

He sat up on the bed, a cold sweat beading on his flesh. He threw off the blanket and felt his heart heave inside his chest. He watched his naked body tremble and recognized the loneliness of judgment.

The scar on his abdomen showed in the dim moonlight inside the bedroom, and his fear turned to anger once he had control.

His body was rocked
into a rhythm of pleasure,
until the movement was calmed
with resoluteness.

Chapter 1

The pen felt like the handshake of an old friend. Mark rolled it between two fingers as if to revive a neglected habit, and then scribbled on a pad the first word that came to mind—*love*. Such an overused word, he thought, but stared at the paper as if to wish that it be granted.

During his adolescence, it was fashionable to require love be applied to whatever aspect of behavior was aspired to—as if the implicit ideals of love would be exerted upon that behavior.

Though in his youth he had been guilty of the nominal use of the term, Mark stared at the pad he had written it on and wondered how he could summon the implicit ideals of love. He leaned back in the desk chair and began to type on the laptop.

◆◆◆

There had been no warning before the windshield burst into shattered glass and metal crumpled with the sound of thunder. Their world began to tumble, as if in the spin cycle of a wash. With the seat belt strap released, his body was jostled against the inside frame of the truck. He turned towards her scream.

In the darkness of the clouded night, amidst the turmoil, he was calmed in her embrace. Time lingered as his thoughts recounted the past.

Not so long ago, his had been a poet's passion, safely bestowed upon the words he wrote. Reality had become a matter of circumstance, not of desire, while vulnerability was a topic for discussion, not a temperament of pride. In his safeguarded emotions, she touched his heart; torrents of pleasure flowed.

Mark retrieved the pen from behind the laptop and twirled it between his fingers as if to prime himself for a review. He studied the words he had written on a topic he had not attempted before, and was baffled by the melodrama. He modified the lines, but he could not get rid of the passion.

Melodrama, he thought, was the exception of our lives, our enigma: it was not with the historical fidelity required for his monthly column. He sat back from the computer screen as if to clear his thoughts with distance. Melodrama, he considered, was our heightened selves; but it was also the language of his Hispanic culture through which he had learned to interpret the world in which he had been raised. It had not, though, become his style.

Mark knew himself as a writer with a penchant for adjectives to enhance the context of his stories; he was determined, therefore, to let the lines remain since it wasn't about himself he wrote.

It might have been the silence in his den, but there sounded a loud echo to his hunger pangs; after all, his last meal had been the night before. He saved the melodrama into the Work-in-Progress folder in the laptop and set out to the market.

◆ ◆ ◆

When he lifted the grocery bags at the checkout counter,

Mark was overcome with a flushed discomfort he had felt multiple times over the last two months. Having described them as *fits*, he became worried on nearing the exit as the feeling progressed to a sense of weakness. Concerned that he could fall, he darted behind a stack of recently-delivered boxes and crouched on the linoleum floor. He waited to recover from the cold sweat that then flooded his skin.

"Do you need some help?" asked a store attendant.

Mark looked toward the voice, focusing on the nametag. "No, thank you... Tony. I feel better now."

Tony grabbed at his elbow and supported Mark as he stood. "Are you sure you're all right? You look a little pale."

"Yes—thanks," he answered. "I can take it from here."

He glared into Tony's eyes as he straightened. The young man's face irked him for the sympathy it displayed, as it seemed to herald the approach of what he dreaded becoming—a feeble, older man.

Irritated at being discovered, Mark felt his strength seep back. He grabbed the cans of vegetables Tony had gathered and headed out the exit door.

Inside the truck, he left the windows closed and briskly rubbed his arms as if for warmth. With the key tightly gripped, he stared at his reflection in the rearview mirror: his brown irises were constricted; strands of his reddish-brown hair hung loosely over the forehead, and the wrinkles about the eyes appeared deeply furrowed in the shadow. He dropped the keys to push back his hair and leaned forward for a closer inspection. *Time grants no reward to the lonely*, he thought in response to his circumstance reflected in the mirror.

Vigorously, he jammed the key into the ignition and

thought of the significance of his recurrent chills. Could it be what some consider male menopause or just the consequence of middle-age physical decay? He rejected both thoughts and let the engine growl his discontent: at forty-two years old, he still felt the spryness of when in his thirties. It could only be hunger, he concluded, and firmly pressed the accelerator. The tires screeched as he drove onto the boulevard.

◆ ◆ ◆

Mark often found it difficult to locate the neighborhood in which he lived among the other nondescript cul-de-sacs that embody the suburbs of San Jose; from an airplane, he knew, these appear much like alveoli of a choked lung. But on that night, he found his home by its apparent neglect.

The dormant grass of his front yard contrasted with the tended lawns of his neighbors, and deep shadows of the waning afternoon were stretched across his driveway. An occasional glare from a passing car shone against the front door he closed behind him. Soon the neighbors would all be home from work.

◆ ◆ ◆

To create characters (as if for a menagerie), Mark often distilled personality traits from the people he met; adapting from his own was unusual. But on that night, he scholarly eyed the perfectly lined groceries he stowed into the cupboards, and those designated for the meal were color-coordinated when laid out to cook.

In contrast to the ingredients he orderly reconciled for preparation, these were merely dumped into the skillet for cooking. Mark figured his favorite condiments of mustard, diced onions, and garlic would make any

Alvarado

meal flavorful and edible.

Enticed by the aroma of the dinner, he sat at the table; but on the second bite of the overdone chicken, he remembered he had brought nothing to drink.

Searching the cupboards, he found only a single bottle of champagne. He carried it to the living room and set it on the table. On inspection of its gold seal and thick colored glass, he presumed the bottle was valuable. He brushed the dust off the glass and recalled his brother's wedding reception: aglow with love, his brother had embraced his bride and handed Mark the bottle. "Hope you find the happiness my wife has brought me," he had toasted Mark and gulped from a second bottle. Champagne foamed on his lips when he kissed the bride.

Mark sat back on his chair and tore at the gold foil. Happiness was illusory, he thought then, for it was not long after their wedding night that his brother's wife had sought the company of another. Like thorns on a crown, she had left clues that led to the revelation. Were it not for her need to hurt, their marriage would have lasted.

After a hearty twist, the cork became ejected across the room, and white champagne suds were sprayed onto his lap. "Whoa!" Mark shouted and quickly sat up. "To the happiness we're all in search of!" He raised his bottle in salutation and then pursed his lips over the foaming gullet. After a large gulp of champagne, he looked about the empty walls of his living room and wondered whether being alone was not a better option.

His moist pants clung uncomfortably to his thighs, but when unzipped, they slipped to the carpet. He stood away from them and approached the window. In the darkened glass, he stared at his reflection and quickly shut the blinds. It wasn't so much for modesty as it was to secure the boundaries.

On second thought, he turned back and separated two slats of the blinds to glance outside. Against a closed curtain of the neighbor's bedroom, on the other side of the fence, the silhouette of a man and a woman appeared at play. He recognized their shadows, but he had not met the couple since they moved in three years before. He let the slats clink shut and returned to the dining table, the bottle cradled firmly to his chest as if for fellowship.

The moisture of the champagne eased the swallow of the chicken, but the meal required a gulp with every forkful. It was not long before he forgot the playful couple next door.

Silence was a condition he enjoyed for its contrast, particularly when he wrote. But when the empty champagne bottle rolled off the table and thumped on the carpeted floor, the silence that followed highlighted the emptiness of his home. He staggered to the adjoining living room and turned the radio to a soft rock station. All the melodies sounded a tone for Sunday drives around the park and all the loves he had left behind. Mark danced instead of crying, until his lonely shadow dropped onto the sofa.

◆◆◆

He reached as to an alarm wakening him from sleep. "Mark?" a familiar voice asked from the other end of the phone. "Is that you, buddy?"

His mouth bore a foul taste when he cleared it to answer, "Yeah."

"Are you all right? You sound drunk."

"Maybe... I am." He blinked his crusted eyelids open and let his eyes roam to assess his location.

"This is Spencer Tate. Are you still asleep?"

"Spencer!" Mark winced at the filtered sunlight in the living room. "What time is it?"

"About ten."

"What?... I've slept all night." Mark eased himself off the sofa and walked to the bathroom, the cordless phone held to his ear.

"Just called to see if you want to go on a commando mission tonight?"

"Yeah, that sounds good." He sat to urinate and thereby lessen the echo from the stream. "How's Kathy?"

"She took the kids to visit her mother. She'll be gone for the rest of the week... How about I meet you at headquarters at seven?"

A frustrated soldier of fortune, Spencer lived his military fantasies vicariously, through the war games he programmed for a living. His distinction was air combat, but it was through research of shoot-outs in the Old West that they had first met. Mark had introduced him to ghost town sites of especially gory battles, from which Spencer had drawn inspiration for a computer game.

There had been a lot of make-believe and not much else in common. In fact, Spencer's pretend-world was drawn up from a place Mark had threaded haltingly and primarily to study the underside of masculinity. But for the convenience of readily available company, they had needed each other. And so, during the few years since, they had become good friends.

"Sounds good—I mean, Roger." Mark shut off the phone.

Mark could not recall their last time out together, but "commando mission" was Spencer's euphemism for a *boys' night out* on the town. More often than not, it was simply going to a bar to get drunk. On emptying his bladder, Mark was reminded of the previous night's binge—and dreaded to repeat it.

◆◆◆

Discipline was the attribute he struggled with most in his quest to write, but anticipation made it much easier to achieve—after a full day of writing, it was precisely seven when he walked into the bar.

The Seoul Lounge was their commando headquarters, not so much for all the drinking they had done there, but for its intriguingly foreign atmosphere. Without much imagination, one could conjure exotic and clandestine schemes on the dragon-decorated bar. As much as Mark could tell, the decor was appropriately Korean.

Randy Durocher tended at the bar, as he had on Mark's previous visits. With his sandy blond hair clipped military style, he didn't appear the seventy-something years he must have been—for all the Vietnam War stories he liked to tell.

"Sue Ye!" Randy shouted toward the back door. "We've got a customer!"

With one foot propped on two boxes of beer, Randy continued a conversation with two men at the far corner of the bar. Cigarette smoke spiraled from a communal ashtray. All were turned toward two players at the pool table. Mark sat on a stool in the middle of the bar.

"What will it be, honey?" Sue Ye asked in a heavily accented voice as she wiped the counter.

"I'm waiting for a friend." Mark pulled away from the edge to give her room and was sure she did not recognize him. "He shouldn't be long. I think I'll wait 'til he gets here."

Sue Ye returned toward the single door in the back. She was attractive, and without a strand of white in her black hair, she seemed twenty years younger than her husband, Randy. Mark preferred when her hair was loose and draped over one shoulder like a silk veil upon her breast, but that night, she had it in a bun. He glanced back to Randy and wondered what the attraction was that bound one to the other.

"Colonel Tate!" Randy shouted toward the front door.

"Sergeant Durocher!" Spencer responded from the doorway. His chest broadened as if to scan the room with his breath, rather than sight. He focused on Mark. "Commander Balcon! I'm glad you kept our rendezvous."

Spencer approached Mark, who stood up to stretch out his hand. Spencer grasped it firmly and led it to an embrace. The whiskers of his groomed beard brushed against Mark's neck.

"It's been a while," Mark said, and hastily stepped back.

"Come yonder." Spencer continued to the empty seat next to the corner man and reached out to Randy for a handshake. His rotund belly seemed to support him as he leaned over the bar. "You remember Mark," he added.

"Sure. How you doin'?" Randy glanced at Mark but quickly turned back to Spencer. "Hey, I have a great new beer for you!" He pulled open the flap of the box he had been resting his foot on. "This is best served *warm*." He poured the beer into a frosted glass.

Spencer took a large gulp. "Oh, man!" He contorted his face in an exaggerated grimace. "This tastes like elephant piss!"

"How did you know?" Randy bellowed in laughter.

"Hey, give my buddy one," Spencer said and to Mark

added, "This is some shit. It'll straighten your pubic hairs!"

"That's a good one!" said the corner man, who faced Spencer. "That'll make it easier to reach for my prick. You never know when you're in for a quick one."

"Hey, man, mine's always on the alert," said the man whose back leaned against Spencer. "They don't call me Dick for nothing!"

The group laughed as Spencer moved away from his stool. He held the bottle at the neck and walked across the lounge. "Hey, Randy, we're going to a table. Your company is too vulgar for my sensitive ears."

"Ooh!" the chorus responded.

"Send Sue Ye over. I think we'll order some of your dog meat," he said and motioned his head for Mark to follow.

"If I was a man who cared, I might be offended by that," Randy replied. "It's the Vietnamese who serve dog. We only have roaches."

Laughter muffled Randy's call for Sue Ye.

"Mr. Tate," Sue Ye said and handed them the menu. Mark recalled she couldn't pronounce *Spencer*. "How you been?"

"Just fine," he said. "You look as lovely as I remember."

"Oh, honey! You talk a lady good!" Sue Ye replied.

"I *do* a woman better!" Spencer stared at her breasts when Sue Ye leaned forward to lay out the silverware.

"Oh, honey, you so nasty!" she smiled and asked, "You want more beer?"

"Mark, finish that." He grabbed his bottle and gulped what remained. "Bring us some Korean poison."

"Ahh, soldier boy, I'm the poison you want!" Sue Ye cackled on her walk back to the kitchen.

Mark scowled as if to force every swallow of the *elephant piss*. When the bottle was empty, he struggled to focus on the elephant label and noticed the *12.5% alcohol by volume*. Was that even legal?

The second beer was easier to drink, but without the alcoholic kick of the first. He gargled with it to cleanse the taste of the elephant feet in his mouth, then ordered dinner. "All I've been doing is working," he continued the conversation. "There's always a deadline, but thank goodness there are readers interested in my articles."

"Are you still getting up to the ghost towns?" Spencer asked.

"Not as often as when we worked on your program. By the way, I like how that game came out."

"Thanks, but it hasn't sold well."

"Oh, no. I suppose I should've *bought* a copy."

"Thanks for nothin', man!"

Mark sat back into the chair for Sue Ye to set their plates. "I think I'll be driving up to Tahoe soon," he said.

"Oh, yeah?" Spencer replied. "Goin' up with a chick?"

"No. I think I'll go alone. Just want to get away."

"Ah. How *sad*." It was Spencer's favorite term for Mark's supposed run of bad luck with women. He dug the chopsticks into a mound of white rice and asked, "Are you seein' anyone?"

"Not now," Mark answered while staring at the chopsticks he gripped between his fingers. He maneuvered the tips, testing their grip.

"Man, you need a woman!" Spencer filled his mouth with a portion of the peppered beef. A morsel slipped from his lips and smudged the white hairs of his beard. "What I would do to be single again." He rolled his eyes and arched one eyebrow. He searched about the lounge.

"Hey, Sue Ye! Come here!"

"You need beer?" she asked and approached their table.

"Yeah, bring us some more…But wait a minute." He held her arm to stop her turning. "You got a lady for my friend?"

"How long?" she asked Mark.

"What?" He lost his grasp of the kimchee cabbage. "No, no, Sue Ye. Not like that!" Spencer retorted. "He needs a *real girlfriend*."

"You got no lady?" she asked, not looking away from Mark.

"No." He tried to recover the cabbage from the table where it had fallen.

"Why not?" Sue Ye was relentless.

"No one loves me!" Mark said, feigning sorrow. He turned to Spencer and shrugged for a distraction.

"Why not? You handsome and got job. Right?" Mark looked at Sue Ye and smiled. "Well, I don't know about being handsome."

"You like boys?" Sue Ye asked.

"Oh, God!" Mark felt a flush on his face.

"Sue Ye! He needs a girlfriend, not an insult!" Spencer interjected.

"I got girl for you." She walked away but soon returned with more beer.

Sue Ye had left a count of her returned visits by a collection of empty bottles on their table. When their heads wobbled just above these, she noisily cleared them to the side and got their attention.

A young Korean lady stood behind her.

"Honey," Sue Ye said to Mark, "this Rose May. She quiet, but beautiful. She give you good love."

Mark pushed himself back from the table. His head

lagged but stopped with a snap. He appealed to Spencer. "Is she serious?" His palms sweated, and his chest quivered.

"Go on!" Spencer answered. His body still drooped above the table, but his stare remained on Rose May. "Go on now, soldier... Don't let me forget that I'm a married man."

◆◆◆

Up a narrow stairwell, a little beyond the restaurant bathrooms, he felt his shoulders scrape the textured concrete walls as he swayed between them. The red lamp at the top of the stairs guided his clumsy steps. A pine-scented cleanser permeated the air.

Her hand, smooth as silk, led him tenderly. Against the dim light ahead of them, she seemed like a swan in her white chiffon dress. Her long black hair, held at the nape of her neck by a wide ribbon, framed her face as she looked back to ensure he followed. Her glance back was all the invitation he needed.

In the room at the top of the stairs was a narrow mattress, raised on a wooden frame. He stood before it and wondered whether they would fit, but smiled at the thoughts of physical contortions that would permit them to share it.

On the opposite wall was a single window, curtained by a purple sheet. A small washbasin stood in a corner by the door. An overhead red lamp reflected its faint light on the linoleum floor.

Mark turned to where she stood waiting at the door and stretched out his arm for her to approach. With her hands upon his chest, he closed his eyes and yielded to her fingers loosening the buttons of his shirt. Her body pressed against his as she unzipped his pants. His clothes glided off him as he reclined onto the mattress.

She stood before him, her arms reaching behind to unbutton her dress, which then dropped to the floor. In her nakedness, she drew his stare. She then unfastened the ribbon that bound her hair, and like the flare of a fan, its black strands fell away from her shoulders. Mark remained silent but drew in a big breath to lay back on the bed.

It was the weight of her body, the feel of her flesh. It was the firmness of her nipples, her moisture, and her scent. It was motion, and it was rhythm… but it was… an imprudent catharsis for his loneliness

The squeal of the bed and the joy of his cry trailed into a quiet he recognized. They lay motionless, one upon the other, yet Mark stared away to the red light. She did not speak English; as far as he could tell, she did not speak at all.

◆◆◆

Besides an occasional neon sign, the strip mall's parking lot was dark. The one light above the rear door of the Seoul Lounge glared on his dull stare. Confused, Mark worked on his orientation, but it was the firmness of the truck's cargo floor on which he lay that captured his attention. He gradually sat up.

There was no traffic on the boulevard and no one else on the lot. He scurried to the far corner of the building; his steps echoed as he approached the wall. Braced against it with one arm, he leaned to unzip his pants. The cold air that stroked his bare skin caused him to quiver. The steam rising from his urine's trail on the wall amused him.

With his weight still supported on his lean to the wall, he felt his shadow thrown against the building when a floodlight shone from behind him.

"Put your hands above your head!" commanded an amplified voice.

Mark stood still, unable to halt the flow of urine. "Oh, shit!" he mumbled to himself.

"Put your hands up, now!" repeated the command.

The elastic band of his briefs snapped back as he yielded. Moist warmth streamed down the inside of his leg.

"Keep them above your head and turn around!"

Mark stared at the ground where a small pool steamed at his feet. Footsteps approached.

"Look up!" thundered the voice.

His antagonist's outline was sharply sketched in the floodlight. Mark balked and stared at his feet.

"Hey, don't I know you?" the voice asked.

Mark raised his hand as a visor, and his eyes strained against the light.

The silhouette turned and added, "Sam, cut the light!"

The warmth faded when the light was turned off, yet sweat formed on his face. The officer's red hair, Mark thought, should help his recollection, but memory failed him. "I… don't know," he replied.

"Hey, Sam, guess what? This guy lives next door to me. Nancy an' me always wondered what he was up to— now I know. He's a *Seoul Man*!"

Mark stammered, "What do you mean?"

"At least he's got taste," said Sam. "They do have the best women in town."

Mark aborted the protest and searched his empty pants pockets. He tried to recall when he had spent the money, but he could think only of Rose May and the feel of her flesh.

"Well, Fredrickson, should we take him in?" Sam moved behind Mark.

"Nah. We've got nothin' on him." In a softer voice, Fredrickson advised Mark, "Stay out of that scene, man. Don't be bringin' no germs to the neighborhood!"

◆◆◆

Mark quietly shut the truck door behind him. A distant dog's bark was the only sound. He stood motionless as a gust of wind stirred the reek of urine from his pants. In the light of dawn, he surveyed the homes of his neighbors: he was the *germ* Fredrickson had warned against—a lonely man.

Inside the townhouse, he prepared to shower, but he wished for—craved—Rose May's fingers to undress him. Naked, he slipped between the bed sheets, but it was the warmth of her flesh he wanted to comfort him. He embraced his pillow and recalled her scent. With his eyes closed, loneliness no longer mattered. In the morning, he would write the tale Rose May would have told him.

Chapter 2

Rose May had once carted granite tailings from deep within the mines in the hills about the town. Calluses on her hands reminded her it hadn't been so long ago. She had stacked the stones into a pyramid, as if in testament to the dream that had lured her west. Yet, from the wooden planks of the boardwalk upon which she now stood, they seemed an obelisk, a memorial to the lives surrendered in a shared illusion. With a steadfast gaze, she pondered on her shattered dreams and the body of her fiancé, buried in a cave-in.

Footsteps on the wooden planks alerted her. A town lady stopped short of the step-off and grabbed at her skirt. She continued onto the road, her dress guarded against the mud. Rose followed, prodding the stem of her umbrella into the mire as if to measure its depth. From her other hand, an embroidered cotton purse swung loosely, brushing her dress, which draped to mid-leg. Colorful pantaloons warmed her legs to the fur trim of her boots.

It was silver she now mined, from the hearts of lonely men. Like the delusions that had brought them to the mines, so they came to her for love. It was not upon stone they set their dreams, but on the fleeting pleasure that she enjoyed giving.

With no more dreams to harvest, only tasks to accomplish, Rose had much business for that afternoon.

"No, no. That's all wrong!" Mark shouted to himself and selected the *Save* command of the program. *Rose May is Korean,* he admonished, then shut down the laptop. *She doesn't even speak English.*

The water kettle screamed from the kitchen and called him away from the den. He waited for the shrill to intensify and watched the steam erupt through its hood. "Go ahead and holler!" he shouted as if goading it to make its wail become his own.

He drank a cup of coffee at the dining table and pushed aside the mustard-stained plate. With his legs stretched out below the table, he felt the champagne bottle roll away. Slumped back in the chair, he focused his stare on the dim light from the adjoining living room and searched his thoughts for the voice of Rose May. But all he could concentrate on were bitter memories:

Ah—how sad, Spencer had said about his plans to travel alone to Lake Tahoe.

Don't bring no germs to the neighborhood, had been the cop's advice.

With his eyes closed, he let out a deep sigh, but the images remained. He rushed to the living room window as if seeking fresh air and swung open the blinds. The neighbor's bedroom curtain was open, but the shadows inside and the silence of the yard told him no one was home. When he leaned back, the blinds crackled with the dissonance of a guitar out of tune. His knees weakened, and his body slid to the floor. He committed to making the trip to Lake Tahoe.

◆ ◆ ◆

From the central California coast, gentle hills rose to become the mountain range bordering the western San Joaquin Valley. In early spring, these hills were carpeted with seasonal green vegetation that turned gold in the summer months. Once over the range and into the valley, a winter fog shrouded farms and funneled Mark's thoughts to tales from *The Grapes of Wrath* and *Tortilla Flats*. He imagined himself on an adventure through Steinbeck country.

A lighted sign abruptly shone through the fog and prompted his attention to the gas meter, which faltered on *Empty*. He drove the truck into the gas station and stopped at the single island of pumps. The wooden building a few yards back, supposedly a coffee shop, appeared weathered—red paint on the trim panels had long ago peeled heavily. An adjoining empty garage stood in darkness with a degree or two in slant. On the front panels, a winged horse was shaded by overlaid white paint.

The station looked to Mark as if it had long ago been abandoned.

The screen door from the coffee shop swung open, and an old man in his seventies stepped out. His visor was turned to the reverse side. He stretched his arm into a stained jacket. The light from inside lit his path toward the pump. "Howdy, son. Want 'er filled?"

"Yes, sir, but isn't it self-serve?" Mark stepped up to the Premium pump.

"Only the interstate guys have enough pumps," he said, reaching for the nozzle.

"Is it far from here?" Mark asked and backed up toward his truck's opened door.

"Don't worry. You won't get it cheaper. Fill 'er up?" he asked again, holding the nozzle with a gloved hand.

Mark hesitated and searched for the unit price. It was reasonable. "Yeah, fill 'er up."

The old man fitted the nozzle into the tank of the truck while a distant mechanical clamor came from the direction of the fog-shrouded fields. Distracted by the noise, Mark sat back in his seat to listen. He envisioned the barren soil being toiled in the wake of a tractor preparing to plant the spring seeds, probably cotton. He hoped to return in summer when the fields of fluffy white crops would be harvested.

"That'll be twenty-five bucks," the old man said and returned the nozzle to its hilt.

"Sure is cold." Mark stood up from the truck and handed him the credit card.

"We got hot coffee," the old man answered and carried the card toward the coffee shop. Mark followed, more to recover the card than for the offer of warmth. At the wall opposite the entry door, a wood stove heated the small dining area. A single fluorescent bulb illuminated the café. Four empty tables were arranged to one side, and a Formica counter lined the other. Mark sat at the counter while the old man searched under it from the serving side.

"I knew I had it here," he said and handled a small metal slab. He straightened and worked the lever to imprint the card. "Shit. I bent it. Don't no one use money anymore?"

"Sorry," Mark replied. "I don't have enough—that is until I get to an ATM."

"Well, how're you gonna pay for breakfast?"

"Breakfast?" Mark asked.

"You look hungry, boy. I'll just add it on the gas bill." The old man removed the jacket and turned to the stove behind him. "Eggs and bacon?"

"Just two eggs, over easy."

"You must be from the city. Here you get 'em whichever way they turn."

Mark smiled at the old man. *Whichever way they turn* was exactly how the old man appeared to live his life.

The pictures on the wall seemed positioned without rhyme or reason. These were front covers of magazines, photos and greeting cards from distant lands at different times. Pens and pencils tied with rubber bands stood clumped inside porcelain cups at the end of the counter. An old ledger was left open, stains of grease on its white pages.

"Where you headin'?" the old man asked, pouring coffee into a cup.

"Lake Tahoe." Mark reclined against the backrest and unzipped his light jacket. The coffee was strong, but it fulfilled the old man's promise of warmth.

"Ain't you takin' a long way about?" He was turned to the stove and seemed to speak to the eggs he tended.

"I suppose I am," Mark answered, reading the John Deere label on the reversed front of the man's hat.

"Never been there myself, but some folk say it's heaven. I got a picture of it somewheres here." He flipped the eggs over.

Mark noticed a yolk break. "Yeah, *I* think it's heaven. I have a cabin there."

"I thought you come from the city," he said and stuffed the toaster with bread.

"I do, but I like to get away."

"I thought you said you ain't got no cash." The old man scraped the eggs from the flat of the stove and dropped them on a plate. "How come you got two homes?"

"Well, I don't have any cash *now*, but I can get some at an ATM." Mark sat up on the chair.

"If you ask me, rich folk oughta carry cash all the time, not a silly gold card that bends when poor folk grabs at it."

Mark noticed a teasing glint in the old man's eyes as

he set the eggs and toast before him. His banter was a prod for conversation.

"I'm not rich, just lucky with a book I got published. It's just that I left in a kinda hurry," Mark said, more to stoke the old man's hankering than to provide any reasoning.

"People are always in a hurry. Even out here. They take the interstate and pump their own gas." He poured himself a cup of coffee. "Now take me, for instance. I was blown out here in a dust storm from the panhandle o' Texas when I was just a boy. My folk are all gone, but I stick around. Never been nowhere farther than half a tank would take me. But I got's all the time in the world to know here well."

Mark was intrigued as to what elements of *here* were satisfying to get to know *well*. He looked about the café and saw only a past. "Where are your children?"

"Got none. Never married." The old man held the cup with both hands and sat on a stool behind the cash register.

"Did you ever want to get married?"

Mark ate the eggs sandwiched with the bread and sipped the hot coffee. The old man's eyes stared at him, pleased that he liked the food.

"I fell in love once. That was a long time ago. I suppose she never worried how far her tank would take her, 'cause she took a trip one day and never came back."

"Did you ever hear from her again?"

"Yeah, she wrote a few times. One of them picture cards is from LA." Like a wand granting a wish, he waved his index finger toward the cluttered wall. "She wanted me to come, and I almost did, but I just couldn't leave where my folk wanted me to be."

He stood up to clean the flat of the stove, with a stare

Alvarado

that seemed transposed in time.

Silence bears its own vigor, and that which followed troubled Mark. The old man's reminiscences mirrored Mark's own pain. He continued with breakfast, pensively watching the burned oil being scraped away.

"Well, that was good," Mark said to disrupt the quiet. He sat back and, to highlight his satisfaction, padded his belly.

"I'm glad you liked it." He cleared the plate away. "More coffee?"

"No, thanks. I better be getting on."

"That's right. You're in a hurry." The old man's hand trembled as he wrote the credit card number on the imprint of the bill. Mark felt a chill when he signed the receipt.

"Take this." The old man handed him a yellowed business card. "I need a new picture from Lake Tahoe."

"*Trapper Garza*," Mark read. "Boy, that's a name with some story."

"Stop by next time you're in the area, and I'll tell it." He followed Mark to the door. "Drive safely. They say it's gonna rain like a cow pissin' on a flat rock."

Mark laughed at the image and zipped up his jacket. He wondered if it ever did rain inside the heavy fog he drove into. Trapper Garza's figure faded from his rear-view mirror.

◆ ◆ ◆

The fog remained dense, and Mark felt as if he was driving in a mineshaft—nothing was visible beyond a few feet. His thoughts seemed as if cast onto the windshield, with images of elephants pissing in beer bottles and cows on flat rocks. *Maybe Trapper Garza was right*, he thought, *to build his world within the confines of half-a-*

tank of gas. He continued on the valley road and worked on acquiring a smile.

From the valley, he ascended the eastern mountain range until abruptly showered with sunlight. He pulled into a vista turnoff that overlooked the vast San Joaquin basin. From on top of a granite boulder, he spanned out his arms like wings and imagined himself in flight above the vestment of clouds.

◆◆◆

The longer route to Lake Tahoe required that he skirt the eastern slope of the Sierra Nevada mountain range. Along the hills rising above the high desert were many abandoned towns that long ago had lured men and women with the prospect of gold and silver. But it was for the stories he imagined that he had long ago been attracted to explore the region.

It was dusk when he reached the road that encircled Lake Tahoe. He took the leg that headed north to the corona of lights from Incline Village. At a bend on the road, he was startled by the flash of red lights. As if in a flashback, he recalled the red light in the small room above the Seoul Bar. Straining his focus against the color distraction, he noticed a silhouette befitting that of Rose May. It took him a moment to register the stalled car on the embankment. He stopped when he glimpsed the driver standing in the beam of the inside headlamp.

Pine scent from the forest drifted through the opened side window. "Need some help?"

Her gloved hands gripped the lapels of her long wool coat as if to shield herself against the cold. The black of her pupils stared back warily. She hesitated, tossing a glance to the back of his truck. "Yes, thank you." She approached the window. "I think I ran out of gas."

"Do you want me to check the engine?" It was an empty offer since he only knew where the battery was, and that was not the problem—all the lights of her Mercedes-Benz were on.

"I'm sure it's just the gas. I've watched the pointer sit on empty for about twenty miles." Her short black hair flared when she sighed in frustration. "This has never happened before."

"I guess it wasn't a half-tank trip?" he said and smiled to himself.

"What?" She gazed probingly at him.

"Nothing. How about I drive you into town and get some gas? I'll bring you right back."

"Thanks. But how about if you drop me off at home? I'll get my neighbor to help me in the morning."

"It'll be no problem," he said.

"I'm too tired. I drove up from Palo Alto, and I just didn't need this." She stomped her foot on the gravel.

"Come on in, then." He reached across and opened the passenger door.

"Let me turn off the lights." She stopped midway to her car and turned to him. "Do you mind if I bring the groceries?"

Mark stepped out and helped with the bags in the trunk; they seemed full of cans.

Once on the road, Mark glanced toward her. The folds of her upper eyelids were full, with a gentle slope. Probably Japanese, he thought. She continued to clutch at the lapels of her coat, so he turned up the heat. "Cold?" he asked.

"No, it's fine. Thanks for stopping," she said to his reflection on the windshield.

"Are you from Palo Alto?"

"No. I was just visiting my fiancé."

"A long-distance relationship?" he said and wondered silently, *wouldn't passion become encumbered by time and distance?*

"It's not that far." She looked briefly toward Mark. "He comes up most weekends."

The groceries sounded a thump when the car hit a curve, breaking their silence.

"Planning on a romantic dinner?" he asked.

"No way." She returned Mark's gaze with a wispy smile. "You can't be romantic when your hands smell of garlic. He has to take me out for that. But I've been with him too long not to know ever to let him get hungry. Plenty of cans in those bags for him to fix himself a meal."

"How long have the two of you been together?" Mark imagined cans of dog food and her fiancé barking but then thought of Susan, who had enjoyed cooking his meals.

"Nine years." She loosened her grip on the lapels and rested her hands on her lap. "Since senior year in high school."

His relationship with Susan had lasted eight months, and by then she was talking of marriage. "Shouldn't you be married by now?" he asked, but immediately questioned his right to be intrusive. *Should marriage always be the end result of love?* he thought to ask but instead quickly added, "Sorry, that's none of my business."

At the city limit was a Welcome sign, but her stare remained fixed on the road ahead. "I suppose there aren't any *shoulds* in our life," she answered nonchalantly, "only *wants*. I guess neither of us has *wanted* to be married."

Susan, he thought, must have been suffocated by his not *wanting*. He had fashioned their relationship by *shoulds.*

He stared at the snow banks encrusted with black dirt that lined the sides of the street. Traffic in town was sparse, yet a signal light guarded the main intersection. He stopped at the red light and glanced to the corner gas station. A man pumped gas as a mist formed with each of his breaths—winter still lingered.

"What do you do?" he asked and, on the green light, continued forth across the intersection.

She sat forward, with hands braced on the dashboard. "Turn right two blocks down. I'm a writer."

"Oh, seriously? What do you write?"

"Haiku."

"In Japanese?"

"No, I write only in English."

"I've read some, but I get lost in its subtleties. My poetic insight doesn't extend beyond cowboy poetry... I'd love to read some of your writings, though."

"It's the second house down." She leaned back onto the seat and jingled keys in her coat pocket. "You can just leave me at the curb."

Shoulds were still much of his character: he drove up the driveway to the wood-paneled townhouse and carried the grocery bags to the front door.

"There, thanks," she indicated, for the bags to be left.

Mark reversed the truck out of the driveway and waited at the curb until she had entered. He supposed she was too guarded a writer ever to offer to share her poems.

◆ ◆ ◆

The desk lamp at the window inside the first house at the bottom of the wooded hill was like a beacon: it heralded the last hill up to his cabin. Mark leaned forward and looked up at its glow; the shadow of the owner always stood behind it, as if to greet him on his return.

Late in rising the following morning, Mark recalled a 70s Motown song that noted comfort being where one hung his hat. In his case, it was his bed that made the difference.

He sat at the dining table for breakfast and gazed out the picture window. It was of a celestine blue that faded into a mist, unfurled over the coastline of the lake. The mountains appeared to jut up into the sky with ribbons of white laced onto their crests. Distant evergreens shadowed the snow, and white streamers soared as clouds above a sapphire glaze that mirrored it all. It was a divine palette that Mark considered his front-row-center on paradise. He made a mental note to send Trapper Garza a picture postcard.

Chapter 3

Exhaust fumes clouded the main intersection where traffic was heavy, as it tended to be on Fridays. These were the locals with errands to run before the weekend swelled with tourists hauling skis and snowboards on the roofs of their ATVs. As he waited for the signal light to change, Mark looked above the vapors to the cloudless sky that appeared free of pollution. He wondered if the Haiku poet had written an interpretive lyric for the vexing hubbub in the intersection.

Driven by the growl in his belly, he felt himself on a mission. It had been more than twenty-four hours since his last full meal, and his cupboards were empty.

◆◆◆

The Maidu were a regional native tribe that had long ago been displaced from their hunting grounds in the Lake Tahoe basin and were eventually forced into extinction. As much as Mark ever discovered, what only remained of the tribe was its name, adopted by his favorite coffee diner on the main road through town.

Inside the diner, slabs of redwood framed the structure, which was not quite a log cabin. It seemed original to the area, from a time when the town forest was fodder for its lumber industry, rather than a backdrop for trophy homes. Though the building had been updated for environmental regulations, the beamed ceiling still harbored an ancient fragrance of burnt wood he always enjoyed on entering.

Maidu Café was more crowded than usual, but he rarely was there for lunch. There were two open tables, while diners in noisy conversation occupied the others. Only one seat remained at the counter, yet two bulky men he supposed were contractors held their ground while he forged between them. He sneaked a view at the newspaper headlines they each held at arm's length. *Continued violence in Sacramento*, warned both. He shifted his gaze to the menu.

"Well, stranger. Welcome back." Her hazel eyes were barely visible above the serrated edges of the papers.

"Emilia!" he said with hesitation. They had chitchatted previously, but Mark was not sure of her name. He attempted to glance at her tag.

"Come on, guys, gimme some room!" Emilia said, looking at his neighbors. Each swiveled on their stool, opening a view of her between their papers. She reached with a coffee pot and filled Mark's cup. "Cream and one sugar. Right?"

"That's right."

"Why bother with the menu? I already know what you're ordering." She scribbled on the order pad.

"How do you know?"

"I'm the Maidu Oracle." Emilia flicked her eyebrows and turned. Her brunette ponytail swung with her as if to punctuate her foretelling. She clipped the order on the kitchen window. He watched her dart about the restaurant, taking orders and delivering food. She was athletic and moved with swiftness and efficiency, but it was her smile that seemed to engage everyone she encountered.

Emilia was tall and lean, but her leg, which showed from the side slit of her peach polyester dress, hinted of her musculature. Her skin was olive, yet darker than his; probably a tan from high-altitude skiing, he conjectured. Mark wondered why she had not been a standout on his previous visits.

He glanced back at her, crouched at a table in conversation with an infant, and tried to guess her age, but quickly turned his gaze back to the neighbor's newspaper. *She couldn't be more than thirty,* he assessed.

"Why so glum?" she asked, on her return with his breakfast. "Here you are—two eggs over easy, home fries, and whole wheat toasts."

"You are amazing!" He felt the contagion of her smile.

"So, you won't doubt me again?"

"No, I don't think I will." He dipped the toast into the soft yolk and hoped for another opportunity to test her skills.

Emilia returned to refill his neighbors' coffee, but held the pot above Mark's cup to ask, "More coffee?" She cleared her throat and, when he returned her gaze, teasingly added, "Or more about me?"

As if on cue, the newspapers crackled and folded away, fully exposing Mark and the flush on his face. He gulped a swallow of the coffee but knew the warm sweat on his forehead was not from its steam. He was relieved when Emilia was called to the service window.

The chatter of a crowd standing at the front door caused him to notice there was no empty table, and Emilia was busy with the rapid turnover of diners. He stared at his plate as if to justify his seat, but a smudge of egg was all that remained on the dish. He wanted to stay but was daunted when the dishes were cleared away. He waited until she was at the cash register.

"I'll be skiing at Diamond Peak tomorrow," she said and collected his money.

"Maybe I'll see you there," he replied and instantly regretted it being noncommittal. He gripped the change and walked out, mindless of the crowd he parted. The screen door clapped loudly behind him, but he was not distracted from his remorse.

Falling snow dusted his way to the truck, but it could as well had been sand for the witless state he felt. While the engine warmed, he sat inside as if in a trance and repeated to himself, *or more about me?* He recited her words as if they would betray a secret. Fumbling with the coins she had given him, he hoped he had left a good tip.

◆ ◆ ◆

Flakes of snow continued to fall silently: the tranquility of winter on spring's debut. Laden with powder, pine branches leaned onto his path. Whorls of white dust formed in the wake of his truck as he drove up the hill. The muted sound of the tires echoed the glide his truck took at each turn on the road; he let the wheels slide as if in dance to a waltz. Without concern, he watched the rear of his truck skirt the snow banks on either side of the road. Driving on the untracked snow, Mark felt as if at play on a carpet of white.

On entering the house, the jingle of the pocketed coins reminded him to solidify plans to ski in the morning.

Outside of the picture window in the living room, the view of the lake was hidden by a misty haze; but on the glass, the vapor from his breath seemed to undulate when he repeated her question: *Coffee? Or more about me?*

The ledge of the fireplace felt cold, but it didn't bother him when he sat to work on the laptop. He typed in her question and searched for correlative content within his files. Unable to find comparable text, he realized it had not been his creation: she had asked it. With her words and smile still fresh in his mind, Mark was tempted to write. Instead, he slammed shut the laptop, determined not to transpose his emotion.

The rhythmic tap of his restless feet on the parquet floor could not keep pace with the tick of the clock. He slumped onto the sofa and fidgeted with the seam of the decorative pillow. He stared at the phone but thought it better not to call Spencer, who more likely would grade his restlessness on the *how sad* scale. Mark decided on the distraction of a workout at the gym.

◆◆◆

Mark had maintained a diligent exercise program which he had labeled the *Executive Plan*: to keep the forty-something gut from sprouting over the belt. It was also a commitment: to be as muscularly fit in his forties as he had been in his thirties.

Twenty years since he began his program, age had not been an issue as to why maintain it. But when the body parts of his peers began to droop like prayer candles, he continued exercising to stave off a similar physical decline.

Mirrored walls encircled the weight room, offering plenty of opportunities to glance at the outcome of his gym efforts. With squinted eyes and a grunt, he spurred his muscle to maximum flex against the weight he lifted; but with a swift glance, he would vainly assess his reflection. *How old is Emilia?* he wondered and, encouraged, moved on to the next exercise.

"Are you done with the bench?" asked a young man whose garments fitted like skin: bulges extended from each joint of his limbs. His torso appeared as if encased in a sheath of muscle.

"I have two more sets," Mark responded and focused on the racked barbells. "But you can work in."

"Thanks, man, but I'll come back." He worked the standing curl bar at the post beside Mark, who started to lift the barbells.

"You're swinging your body," the young man said into the mirror and continued with his curls. "You'll do better to decrease the weight and maintain good form."

"Thanks. I guess I am." *And your diaper needs changing,* Mark added under his breath, but took up the lighter barbells. Without swing, he finished the set and walked off to the opposite side of the room.

An older woman worked the thigh adductors, while Mark used the adjacent quadriceps machine. The roam of their eyes met on the fronting mirror. "Hi… It's amazing what we have to go through to fight off age!" she said.

He replied with a snicker that he meant more to be directed to the young weight lifter. "Yeah," he answered and, curious about her sensuous exercises, asked, "What muscles are you working?"

Given the wrinkles on her face, Mark thought she was in good shape for her age. But in the black leotards, she appeared from a time long past and not very attractive.

"Thigh adductors and the pubococcygeal muscles," she said and separated her legs to push on the weight.

"What do they do?" he asked.

"Heighten sexual arousal."

Mark looked to his thigh muscles in contraction and quietly cleared his throat. "Oh?... That sounds... interesting."

The woman stopped mid-motion; the apparatus kept her thighs wide apart. "Have you ever heard of Tantric Sex?" she asked as if offering an investment opportunity.

He looked at her reflection in the mirror and shrugged. "No. Is that something like tawdry sex?"

"Quite the contrary." She released herself from the contraption and stood to look at Mark. "You might consider it experiential divinity through the practice of physical intimacy."

"I suppose you're not Catholic."

She chuckled and released the rubber band that held her long, zebra-patterned hair in a bun. She squatted briefly to stretch her legs and reached into her bag. "Here's my card. If you're interested, my husband and I have an introductory workshop every week."

"Thanks." He read from an unadorned white card, *Carol & Andrew Weber, Tantra and the Art of Intimacy.*

"He's not the music man!" she added, then went into the women's dressing room.

Mark stared at the print on the card as if further explanation was coming. Susan had complained that their relationship lacked intimacy. Had he known it was as simple to learn as flexing his pubococcygeal muscles, he might have acted on her demand.

"Hey, man!" The bodybuilder interrupted his thoughts with a tap on the shoulder. "Can you spot me?"

"Sure." Mark followed to the bench press and safeguarded the card in his pocket. He wondered where divinity factored into intimacy, and whether it was why he fell into hell on the breakup with Susan.

"Give me a boost. I'll do about three reps," the bodybuilder requested.

Mark glanced at the weights at either end of the bar and thought it was more than he could ever lift if the bodybuilder failed. He hesitantly approached the head of the bench when he realized there was no one else in the gym to replace him.

The bodybuilder bellowed, and his face became flushed when straining to lift the weights.

"Push it, man! it's all you!" Mark repeated what he had heard other spotters shout.

"Hey, thanks for the spot," the bodybuilder said with his hand out for a handshake. "I'm Shannon."

"Sure. I'm Mark." He returned the handshake. "I'll be around if you need another spot."

◆ ◆ ◆

The storm passed while he was in the gym, and bright sunlight was left in its place, giving him hope for many good days of skiing. On his deck, and from the overhang of the roof, water dripped from melting snow. In the shade, an icicle was thawed into a silent cascade.

Inside, he sat on the perch of the fireplace and lifted the laptop in preparation to type. He studied his previous search and opened a new screen to retype what she had asked: *Coffee? Or more about me?* But his fingers felt frozen when hovering over the keyboard: he wanted his imagination to end at her words. *Not this time!* he shouted silently and selected *Delete*.

Chapter 4

Darkness slipped through the windows during the two hours he napped. The blackness in the room made Mark wonder if his eyes were fully open. With the lamp on, he noticed a business card on the tabletop. It was the invitation Carol at the gym had given him. He read over the tagline, *Tantra and the Art of Intimacy*, and considered how he had failed Susan. His gaze wandered to his laptop, sitting closed on the perch of the fireplace. It was into it he had stowed away the courage to work on their relationship.

He jumped up from the couch and flung the afghan from over his shoulder to cover the laptop: he wanted a second chance.

In the distance, between the trees and at the edge of the lake, he saw the sparkle from the casino lights. As gambling had often been a pleasurable pastime, he considered it was a good place to set a new course.

◆ ◆ ◆

New directions, he supposed, required a change in perspective; and for that purpose, he carefully examined his reflection in the vanity mirror: salt-and-pepper whiskers shadowed the sharp angles of his jaw; the hairline receded from the edge of his temples; and wrinkles showed where he had not felt smiles. At one time he would have considered himself appearing as a timepiece, with every stroke of an hour featured on his face. But, after a steamy shower, he watched how the water dripped from his hair and slid down the muscles of his chest—Mark became startled by his arousal.

After a shave, he combed over the bare areas of the hairline. He proceeded to put on the most fashionable of the hand-me-downs he kept in storage. After brushing the flat of each black sneaker on his opposite calf, he marched past the full-length mirror without giving it a second glance.

◆◆◆

At the Hyatt Hotel/Casino parking lot, located within a grove of tall ponderosa pine, he put on the woolen sweater Susan had given him three years previously. On the attached Christmas card, she had bid him farewell. The sweater had remained in its colorful wrapping, under the tinseled tree, until the dried pine needles became a fire hazard.

With a deep sigh, he took a whiff of pine scent and glanced up to the canopy of the forest. He hoped that Susan's life since had gone her way.

He pushed open the glass door, and the warm air that rushed against his face was heavy with the strong smell of tobacco smoke and alcohol. Inside the lobby, he felt as if he had walked into daylight, with all the light that flooded him. The decorations in the room were standard, but the focus was on the large rock fireplace in which tall flames leaped up from a gas log.

Guests clumsily traipsed around each other while toting skis and luggage. Others greeted friends with jovial shouts that touted their weekend parties had begun.

Waves of cheers and laughter from the adjoining casino periodically distracted the newly-arrived. One-armed bandits, dispersed throughout the spacious gambling floor, rang alarms in proclamation of rewards given to hopeful gamblers. The loud metal clang of generously-dispensed winnings coaxed stragglers into the dim casino. Overhead neon lights illuminated aisles of opposing blackjack tables. Enthralled, Mark entered the casino.

It was busier than he had hoped, but there remained one table with no one else at play. He sat at the end stool and counted out his fifty dollars onto the velour tabletop. He thought the dealer, appearing to be in his thirties, had a familiar look that he could not place.

"How are ya?" the dealer asked and gathered the single deck of cards that was splayed in a semi-arc, face up, on the tabletop. "Haven't seen ya here for a few months."

"Hope these empty chairs aren't a sign of your skill," Mark said. He was surprised at being remembered, and glanced at the nametag to respond, "I was here last month, Tom—and even won. I missed you then. Hope you'll be as generous tonight."

"Well, let's see what we can do." After he exchanged Mark's money into five-dollar chips, Tom shuffled the cards. "Where's your lady?"

"I'm here alone." He shifted on the stool. Tom had confused him for another player. "It might have been someone I met here."

"Yeah, this is a good place to meet chicks." Tom handed him the cutting card.

"I feel the luck," Mark said and inserted the plastic wedge into the middle of the deck.

"Well, let me dish it out to you, then." He began to deal. "First card up is a Queen of Hearts. A very good sign. It means you're in luck for romance."

"I'll settle for that." Mark leaned forward and picked up his two cards. "A perfect blackjack!" he cried out and turned the spades for display. "Is this an omen, or what?"

"I guess the Queen of Hearts foretells all good fortune. After all, it costs money to entice a fine woman."

"I'll settle for the money if you keep dealing the same hand," he replied with a chuckle but was also hopeful on the prospect for romance. As he gathered his winnings, Mark let his eyes roam the room. "There are some beautiful ladies here tonight."

"Yes, sir... I'm like a hummingbird in a field of roses." Mark noticed the gleam in Tom's blue eyes as he continued, "I have to admit, though, the best nectar is always at home."

"Well, Tom, it's pretty dry in my home garden." He picked up two face cards to the dealer's six upcard, but the tease of a winning hand did not distract him from the expectation Tom would offer some shallow sympathy.

"Man, that's only temporary." Tom dealt himself a breaking card. "I have a feeling your fortune will change tonight. That's what these cards are telling me... Wanna drink?"

"Sure." Mark thought he needed an elixir for courage and suspected alcohol was not it. He remembered his staggered gait going up the stairs following Rose May.

Tom raised his hand, and as quickly, a hostess approached Mark from his right. "Would you like something from the bar?" She stood sidelong; her flank rested against the cushioned border of the table. On the palm of her right hand, leveled to her bosom, she held a tray. Her breasts were cradled snugly in an uplifted, low-cut dress.

"I'll have a beer." Mark felt the warmth of embarrassment when he realized his stare was directed elsewhere than her face. With ballistic motion, to avert a challenging glare, he turned his attention to the table and impulsively split two face cards.

"What kind of beer would you like?" She reached for an empty glass to the left of Mark and lightly brushed his arm with her breast.

Beads of sweat formed above his eyebrow and threatened to drip. He wiped his forehead with the palm of his hand, but his stare remained resolute on the cards. "Bud Lite would be fine."

"That comes on tap—or would you prefer a bottle?"

If preferences were options, he would rather the earth swallow him. "Bottle," he answered with finality.

He listened for her departure as he watched Tom deal a six onto his first face card and a three on the second. Too worn out to struggle, he stayed on both hands.

"Man-o-man, she caught you with your eyes down her dress… but you looked like she had you by the balls," Tom said as he dealt himself five small cards that broke the dealer's hand. "Yes, sir! You looked white all the way into the brown of your eyes… My man, you are in definite need of a good lay." Tom paid both hands. "And I'm happy to contribute to that cause."

Mark's chuckle flourished into a belly laugh as he recognized a camaraderie developing with Tom. With a dealer's bet placed on the table, the cards continued in his favor.

"All right, man. I think we have something here," Tom happily stacked his winnings from the dealer's bet.

The hostess reappeared and assumed the previous pose. Mark noticed she was about his age. The bottle of Bud Lite she carried was placed against the cushioned rim of the table and, on her turn, the warmth of her breast brushed his arm. In tandem, Tom and Mark glanced at each other and snickered. The hostess seemed puzzled, but her dark brown eyes brightened when he dropped a tip onto her tray.

"Thanks," she said and walked away.

A second dealer—a female, slim and blonde—arrived from behind Tom and tapped him on the shoulder. He instantaneously splayed out the deck of cards face up on the table. "Thanks for the bets, sir," he said and waved his hands to the security cameras in the ceiling before gathering the winnings from the dealer's bet. "It's that time. The home nectar awaits me," Tom said with a wink to Mark.

"Thanks for the fortune telling." Mark pushed some additional chips toward him.

"Hey, good luck, man," Tom said. "Remember, the Queen of Hearts reigns over romance, and she ain't gonna let your balls get swolled up."

Tom dropped the chips at a nearby repository, then patted the back of a floor supervisor with whom he shared some laughs. After a short conversation, Tom continued with a pepful stride toward the *home garden*.

"Are you making a bet?" the new dealer commanded, more than inquired. She shuffled the cards and held them with both hands close to her chest. With a glare directed at the table where his bet should have been, she appeared more like the Jack of Spades wielding justice.

Prompted by her stare, he placed a bet where it was

directed, but held back a chuckle he would only share with Tom. "Are you lucky tonight?" Mark asked.

"I don't know. I'm just beginning my shift." She dealt herself an ace card up. "Insurance?" she asked and finished the rest of her deal, unfazed by the apparent threat her upcard imposed on Mark.

He took a gulp of the beer for temporary relief of his increasingly dry throat and peeked at his hidden cards—a thirteen was not much to insure. He retreated his hand to the cushion of the backrest and gripped it for an expected financial fall. "Do you feel lucky?" he asked.

"If I could feel lucky, I wouldn't be standing here," she replied and turned over her down card for validation. "Blackjack."

"Suzanne from Kansas," he read from her nametag as if to call out his nemesis. She may have jabbed the first blow, Mark thought, but he was intent on battle. He stared at her hands as she restarted the match.

Suzanne was lean and tall, appearing to have once been attractive. The shriveled skin of her face was that of a nervous smoker. Her white-blond hair was a product of overindulgence in bleach. The only thing Kansas about her was the old-maid twist in which she held her hair. She gripped the card deck with authority and seemed determined to devastate Mark's treasure. If it weren't for the beer so generously dispensed, he would have sought battle elsewhere. It was with relief he welcomed another player.

The young woman, probably in her mid-twenties, sat on the end-stool opposite Mark. With her left hand held close to her body at the level of her waist, she guarded a roll of one-dollar chips. With her other hand, she brushed back sandy brown strands of hair and quickly glanced at Mark. Her stare became focused on the cards

Suzanne prepared to deal.

"Place a bet," Suzanne directed, without a welcoming tone.

"I'm sorry." The newcomer appeared startled as she gathered two chips to place on the table marker.

Simultaneously, Mark and Suzanne turned to the placard at the end of the table and recognized the edict of a two-dollar minimum bet for their table. Suzanne began to deal, but after a few hands, it was clear the new player had shifted the luck to Mark's benefit, but not her own. With sympathy, he watched her frequent discard of losing hands.

As in a turning tide, the emerald in her eyes began to glisten on a cascade of cards, and he tried to imitate the span of her smile when she cried out, "Twenty-one!"

When Suzanne paid out her winnings, the new player's smile of triumph gradually ebbed into a conspiratorial grin. She turned to Mark as if to enlist an accomplice.

"Congratulations," he responded in surrender to whatever plot she was scheming.

"It looks like you're doing well." She glanced at his chips, stacked against the cushioned border of the table.

"Suzanne was ripping me apart until you brought me good luck," he responded.

While the dealer continued undaunted, Mark watched the young woman's hands. Folded on the green velour, they seemed to guard her chips against Suzanne's apparent resolve. Her long, manicured nails mirrored the neon lights in their gloss of clear polish. She wore no ring, neither of commitment nor for embellishment. Her lack of ostentation attracted him.

"Would you like another card?" Suzanne sternly asked Mark.

Jolted from his musing, he straightened in the chair and reached for the dealt cards. His hand lightly slapped the glass of beer and a ripple spilled onto the table. "Oops, sorry about that… I'll stay."

Suzanne wiped the table clean, but as if to avenge his effort, she turned an ace upon her exposed Queen of Hearts. "Blackjack," she said casually.

"Oh, no!" his co-conspirator whined. "I worked hard for those cards. Suzanne, how could you do that to me?"

Mark counted out an unnatural twenty-one in the cards his co-conspirator had laid out. Suzanne deftly swept away the losing cards. The young woman stared with disbelief at the spot where her cards had once been.

Mark considered a sympathetic overture but was startled when she spoke, "Can you imagine? Losing that hand with a twenty-one?"

"I told you she was mean," he said and sipped his beer. "Let me buy you a drink to alleviate the pain."

She smiled, an attractive dimple forming on her cheek. "That's quite generous. A kind offer like that cannot be refused," she responded in play to the house-complimentary drink.

While Suzanne shuffled the deck, Mark called out to the hostess attending the adjacent table. "Suzanne has left us with a bad taste. Please bring us all a salvaging drink!" he said with a theatrical motion of his hand.

The hostess approached and assumed her pose. "What will the lady have?" she asked, only partly turned toward her.

"Tomato juice, please," the young lady requested.

"As in Bloody Mary?" the hostess asked.

"As in plain tomato juice," she countered.

The hostess brushed his arm on her turn. "Rather attentive, isn't she?" he said after her departure. "Driving home tonight?"

"No. I'm staying at the hotel. I'm just not much of a drinker." She held the cutting card Suzanne had handed her and measured it against the deck. With whimsical determination, she forced it in at the selected depth. "There. The luck will now be on our side of the table."

"Good cut," he said to wish her a good hand. "You don't drink alcohol?"

She picked up the newly-dealt cards. "It's not that I don't drink. It just depends on the occasion." She glanced away to a decorative neon light on the ceiling. Looking bemused, she bit her lower lip, as if to restrain a recent memory. "There's nothing like a Chardonnay before a romantic dinner."

"Sir, are you playing this hand? And don't knock the beer." Suzanne interrupted his imagining of a white-clothed dinner table sprinkled with candlelight, and the dimple of her smile refracted through the crystal of the wine glass.

"Oh, I'm sorry again." He rushed to look at his cards. "I think I've had too much beer… but not enough good cards." Suzanne dispensed a nine card to match the concealed twelve. "Perfect," he responded but felt penitent when he noticed the young lady's losing hand.

She glanced at his winnings. "I would think that stack of chips could buy you a very lavish romantic dinner."

The hostess returned with the tomato juice, which she left by the dollar chips. Mark gulped what beer remained and took the glass the hostess handed him. Her breasts brushed his arm on her turn to another table.

"How romantic can dinner for one be?" he hesitantly asked.

"In the spirit of romance, cherished thoughts keep our company," she replied without sympathy.

"Then let's drink to wine and romance." He raised his glass, watching that the beer did not spill.

"And to all things we share." She raised hers in response.

"Excuse me for interrupting the poetry," Suzanne interjected, "but aren't we here to play blackjack?"

They broke out in laughter.

From the stage beyond the slot machines, a band started playing Eighties soft rock music, which seemed to turn their luck. The cards Suzanne dealt his accomplice began to be more rewarding. Her enthusiasm on greeting her winnings was infectious and heartened Mark to take his losses while tapping his feet to the music.

Whether because of the music he was enjoying or from the work of Tom's Queen of Hearts, Mark felt an encouragement whenever his accomplice offered him attention. He waited for the right moment to pursue the appropriate topic.

"Hi, lady and gent. I'm Oscar, and I've been sent to take your money." Mark had not noticed Suzanne step back and the new dealer step in. With the boy-next-door looks, he was bundled with charisma. His black hair gleamed almost purple in the neon light. "And what are your names?" he asked.

"Belinda," she answered, her eyes focused on Oscar's hands while he shuffled the cards.

"And a beautiful Southern belle ye be! There ain't too many Belindas in Nevada."

"I be from Louisiana, with a mortgaged sugar-beet plantation; and if you be a gentleman, only the best of cards you'll give to me," she played along with her designated role.

"Whoa, my lady! A top order that would be; but for

the sparkle in your eye, my soul I would give… But to do your part, take this magical card and split the block." He handed her the cutting card, which she inserted into the deck. Her eyes did not waver from his stare. "Consider your wish granted!" he said and raised the deck of cards to his heart.

Oscar dealt Mark the first card. "Are you Miss Belinda's fortunate escort, or the evil banker seeking her fortune?"

Dumbfounded by their interplay, Mark felt witless. "Neither… but maybe lost in space."

"That's good, I think," Oscar said, and feigned seriousness with a frown. "'Tis better to be lost in space… hmm, than never to have loved at all?"

"Oh, my god, you're a riot!" Belinda laughed.

Snubbed by their rapport and eventually by the cards, Mark decided to play his last chip. A Queen of Hearts accompanied a Jack of Spades—not enough of a hand for the unnatural twenty-one Oscar dealt himself.

◆ ◆ ◆

Mark walked the aisle heavy-footed and headed toward the casino's exit. Periodic shrills affirmed other gamblers' claims to luck and drew his attention. As if bewitched by the cacophony of dispensed coins into metal bins and the luster of the neon lights, Mark was even then tempted to pursue other games of chance, where the Queen of Hearts could intercede.

He wondered what tortured him more, being spurned by luck or by Belinda's attention. He shoved his hands deep in his pockets and gripped tight the coins Emilia had given him. Trusting that the Queen of Hearts would inevitably prevail, he walked out of the casino.

Chapter 5

Success requires creativity and activity was a motivational slogan he had conceived and placed to scroll across the computer screen. It was a prompt to forestall writer's block. But on that morning, after his casino venture, Mark mentally recited the slogan to spur him out of bed.

With the blinds partly opened, a splintered sunshine was sprayed across his uncovered body. From the warmth it generated, he realized the sound of dripping water coming from outside was more likely from melting snow rather than rainfall.

It was the ring of the phone at his bedside that jolted him out of bed. "Hello?" he answered expectantly.

"Marco?" a heavily accented voice asked.

"Hola, Mami!" he replied, comforted by his childhood greeting. He rested back on the pillow.

In melodramatic Spanish, his mother continued, "I've been calling you every day. I've been so worried; I thought something had happened." The English translation depended on the emotion she would inflict on each syllable.

He listened to her conversation and realized his envy

at the passion she placed on the mundane. Her love was apparent by the energy required to sustain the drama, and this comforted him, even with her scolding. Mark wished to tell her why he drove up to the lake, but could only muster single-word responses.

"*Te quiero*," his mother said on her goodbye, which contrasted painfully with the emptiness he felt on hanging up the phone. His body began to tremble until he focused on the scar of his abdomen—he had to take control.

Recalling Emilia handing him the change, Mark regretted his non-committal. As if sparked by a thought, he jumped out of bed and, at the window, drew the blinds wide open—it was the perfect day to ski.

◆ ◆ ◆

He slipped on the ice in the parking lot and was reminded of how long it had been since his last ski trip. Reassuringly, he padded the bulky gear he wore and headed to the first lift.

With only a few skiers on the slopes, the lift line was short. Mark defiantly passed the marker for the *singles' queue* as there was no one to care he was alone. He waited in the doubles' line.

"How's it goin'?" welcomed the lift attendant, as he continued to shovel snow off the ramp.

Mark scuttled to position and nearly tripped on his crossed ski tips. With his balance quickly regained, he flexed forward and projected his buttocks to the oncoming chair. "Looks like a great day for skiing," he said.

"Watch the chair to your left," the attendant cautioned him, who prepared to receive it from the right. At that moment, the rim of the seat crashed against the back of his thighs and propelled him forward. He fell slumped into the chair but managed to hold on. Lifted above the incline of the slope, he glared at the growing chasm below his skis and gradually accommodated himself into the chair.

A gentle breeze only heightened the silence that greeted him at the summit. No other skier followed him off the lift, so he slowly wandered to the edge of the mountain. As if on a platform above the world, he glanced at the vast panorama. To the east was the Carson Valley, an earthen basin that appeared hemmed by jagged desert mountains. To the west were gentle streams of snow that appeared to flow into the thicket of the pine forest. Beyond the canopy of green was Lake Tahoe, a shimmer of silver in the late morning sun. The cloudless sky above it was a celestine blue.

With prudence (an imposition of mortgages and credit card debt), he cautiously skied on a gentle downhill course. At a black diamond sign, he stopped to reconsider. From the ledge where he stood, the experts' run ahead seemed a vertical drop. But before he had overcome his caution, the swooshing sound of a skier approached from behind. He stared at her form as she continued, without pause, down the slope he gawked at.

Like with hummingbird wings, her bright green jacket was fanned out by the wind. Her ski pants fitted snugly on the curves of her hips, which swiveled deftly on each of her turns. Like a dancer, she held the poles at arm's length and kept rhythm to the motion of her body: her weight shifted from hip to downhill hip as she took each mogul at its crest. *Surely,* he thought, *she was flying above the snow!*

Her triumphant shout at the bottom of the run prodded Mark to follow. As if dragged by the poles that trailed him, his arms floundered, and the skis sounded gritty when they scraped the face of each mogul. Where she had grace, he prayed for survival. But he imagined himself at dance in her wake.

Back at the base of the hill, a small crowd had lined up for their turn on the chair lift. To the side of the roped area, three skiers were joined in jovial conversation. The one facing away was the skier in green. Her two companions were cliché *ski-jocks*: tall and brawny, with sun-bleached brunette hair. On their snow-tanned faces, they wore reflective sunglasses. With red ski-patrol jackets, they could have been twins.

Mark strained to hear her voice, but she remained turned away from him. He positioned himself to snoop on the conversation, but was rattled by their laughter. He shifted his focus to the couple in line ahead of him. They remained embraced in what seemed a perpetual kiss. Mark scuttled to the singles' line.

"Are you single?" he was asked from behind when his skis got tangled on the rope between the queue lines. Mark turned to face his questioner and recognized Emilia, the skier wearing green. "Oh, my—it's you!" he answered.

"Mark! I had hoped you would come. Can I ride up with you?" She skated to his side.

"By all means." He struggled to free the trapped ski and then scooted to make room for her. He glanced behind her and was delighted the twins had not followed. "I was behind you down that last run, but I couldn't keep up. You're a great skier!"

"Thanks. Did you take 'Diamond Back'?" she asked and moved forward in line.

"Yeah, but not with the grace you did."

"I love those six-foot moguls. I've been skiing them all morning."

Emilia brushed her lips with chapstick, and the glove

Alvarado

she removed fell at his feet. Mark reached for it, and as he did, the skis slid into those of the couple still in an embrace.

"Oops, sorry!" he said, but the couple didn't seem to have noticed.

"Thanks." Emilia took the glove and smirked toward the undisturbed couple. She added, "I didn't see you on the slope."

"Of course not. You blew me off at the top of the hill."

"I'm sorry. I can be that way: I get so focused when I'm having a great time that I don't pay much attention to anything else," she said, "and it's such a beautiful day."

The couple ahead remained in embrace, even as they continued to the boarding platform. The attendant finally got them to separate for the on-coming chair.

"Maybe they're just trying to keep warm," Mark smiled as he and Emilia took their positions.

"Don't forget to take the chair from the left," the attendant cautioned Mark. Then to Emilia, he asked, "How was the run?"

"It was great. Have you been on it today, Jerry?" she asked and positioned herself into the moving chair.

"As soon as I get off work," he answered and held the chair for Mark.

"It seems everyone knows you around here." Mark settled himself comfortably in the chair as it lifted them above the trees.

"I sometimes work the ski-patrol, so I've gotten to know most of the regulars. Did you go to Maidu for breakfast?"

"No, I had cereal at home," he said, and lifted off his sunglasses, hoping she would likewise.

Emilia turned and glanced at him through her sunglasses. "I'm really glad you came up."

"So am I." He said but could not think of anything more to add. He shivered with the cold of a gentle breeze as the chairlift ascended just above the crown of the inclined forest. "How long has it been since you were that deeply in love?" Mark directed her attention to the embraced couple ahead.

"You mean *in lust?* Probably when I was their age, in high school," she answered. "How about you?"

Lust was from a wellspring of emotions he often dipped into for creating conflicts among the characters he wrote about, but it was not an emotion he could remember experiencing himself. He glanced to Emilia who seemed to be spying ski runs for her next challenge.

"Probably high school as well," he said to his feet.

"Which do you mean, lust or love?" she asked and lifted her glasses to make eye contact.

When her hazel eyes gazed at him, he understood why melting snow drips. "Lust, I suppose… Love is way too complex."

"Love is no more complex than we are; lust is what we learn to become," she said, and nothing else.

Had he lost her? Mark stared away to the forest below them. The trees were bent leeward and seemed stunted at the higher altitude.

Vestiges of a recent storm were evident on the dark pine stalks, which were embossed white with fury-blown snow. A chill wind continued to sweep the ice crystals that molded themselves to the pine. At the crest of the mountain, the summit station came into sudden view.

"I'm taking one more run before lunch… Follow me!" she said after they skied off the lift to where he had earlier stood.

"The whole world at a single glance!" Emilia's outstretched arms spanned the view from the Carson Valley to the lake. "Here, there's no limit to nature; nor should there ever be on any of us."

Mark followed her on a stream of snow into the thicket of the forest. He listened for the music Emilia's body swayed to, and heard it in the wind that opened her wings and brushed against his face. With the poles gripped at the handles, he danced on the moguls and roared in triumph when he came up to Emilia at the bottom of the run. He sprayed a rooster-tail of snow at her legs on his rapid stop.

She turned away from the flying snow but then responded, "Freedom feels good... but hunger doesn't. Let's go for lunch."

A narrow path led them through the forest and below the overhang of tree branches. Chunks of snow fell when their shoulders brushed against them. She stopped at the lodge and waited for Mark, who followed far behind. "Did you fall? You've got snow all over you."

"No. You blew it all on me."

"I did not... Did I?" she laughed and brushed the snow off his shoulders. "I guess I got even. Are you hungry?"

Before he answered, she had unstrapped her skis and spiked them into a snow bank. Her boots sounded harsh on the grated floor as she stepped into the lodge. Mark rushed to keep up and jumped the two steps to the deck, but slipped when he landed. His arms flailed to catch the rail.

"Good move!" she shouted from the door.

"You liked that, heh? I just don't want to be left in the cold." He continued into the lodge.

Two patrons sat at a long bar opposite from where

Mark and Emilia had entered. Beer bottles at the ready, they were in a spirited conversation with a female bartender.

"Emilia!" the attendant called out.

"Norma!" Emilia responded from the door.

Mark followed her across the wooden floor and pivoted around empty log tables. Off the end of the bar was a large stucco fireplace; above its mantle, were two nine-point antlers. A strong odor of spilled beer supplanted the absence of sunlight.

"Let's eat outside," he whispered to Emilia as they approached the bar.

"Well, girl! I was just telling these guys about you." Norma motioned to the two at the table. They looked up as if being called upon but kept a tight grip on their bottles, as if to a gearshift. Their loose plaid shirts gave them away as snowboarders.

"What about? My Maidu oracle skills?" she asked and winked her eye at Mark.

"These guys are engineer students at Berkeley. I was telling them you study Native American prayers there."

"Well, it's not for the prayers that I go," she answered. In a more casual tone, she added, "But we're hungry. I'll take a Swiss cheese sandwich," then pointed to the display refrigerator, "and that fruity punch."

"I'll have the same," Mark added and reached for the clipped dollars inside his breast pocket but stooped to pick up a dropped glove. Emilia paid for her order.

"No, no. Let me!" he protested and handed Norma the cash.

"Let's make it some other time," Emilia said and gathered her food into her forearm. She headed for the side door.

"Are we on for Steamers tomorrow?" Norma called

before Emilia walked out. "You know Victor will be there?"

"I'm planning on it," Emilia said without stopping.

The deck jutted out above an escarpment of boulders, and the forest enfolded it at the periphery. With the shadow of trees parted as if on curtain call, a central vista of the lake was on display. The diners were turned to the sun, like marigolds on a prairie. Many of the men had bared their chests, and women wore bikini tops.

"Do you mind if we share your table?" Mark asked the single diner at the only open table. She moved to the opposite end in response.

Even before he was settled on the bench, Emilia had begun to eat her sandwich. "I'm so hungry and I was shaky there for a while. They say the last run is always the most dangerous, and I can see why."

"Well, you seemed in pretty good control." He removed his sunglasses as his back was to the sun. He enjoyed the sheen of natural light on her face.

"Thanks for offering to pay; but I was heading here anyway. It wouldn't be fair," she said after a few bites of the sandwich.

"No problem, but I'm in debt for you showing me the way. I'll take you up on that some-other-time request," he said.

With an impish smile, she asked, "Will it be breakfast?"

"Why?" He leaned forward; his elbows rested on the table as he focused on the curious movement of her eyebrows.

"It's all I've ever seen you eat," she answered.

"Not quite." He bit into the sandwich. "Now you've seen me eat lunch… What other of my idiosyncrasies can I dispel?" A flush warmed his forehead when he considered the *germs* the neighbor cop had warned him against.

"You always order the same breakfast," she added.

"So, your powers as an oracle are based solely on probability." Feigning indignation, he added, "I'm feeling a little self-conscious."

"Don't be. I've enjoyed watching you, especially when the yolk drips from your toast. It's cute how you dip the tip of the napkin into the water glass to wipe it off your shirt."

"Oh, God!" He straightened to look away, and with a quick swipe of his hand, swept the crumbs off his mustache.

He noticed one of the red-coated twins emerge from the lodge. Emilia touched his hand that gripped the corner of the table as if to respond to the sudden gloom on his face. "I'm only kidding."

Mark hoped the exhaled air from his deep sigh would blow away the intruder, but instead, it seemed to lead him to them.

"Emilia!" the twin cried out.

She loosened her hold of his hand and turned back. She hesitated before a response. "Victor!"

"Why didn't you tell me you were coming to lunch?" he asked with a brusque Boston accent. He maneuvered himself to the edge of the bench on which Mark sat, their shoulders buffeted against each other. Mark scooted to make room and neared the lone diner, on whose table they had intruded. She stared away from the threesome but yet seemed eager to eavesdrop on their conversation.

"I thought you and Bob were taking a patrol run," Emilia replied. Then to Mark, she offered, "This is Victor Celeste."

"Pleasure to meet you." Mark tightened his handshake against the lie. "I'm Mark Balcon."

The lone diner left the table stealthily, and Mark wondered whether he should follow. He looked across to Emilia. Her sunglasses were perched on her forehead, and her eyes pleaded for him to stay.

"Bob was called away to the infirmary. Someone twisted an ankle or something like that. I decided to take a run and hopefully catch up with you." Victor's gaze was as intent upon Emilia as on his chatter. "Maybe we could go down the Gulch later. Bob went down it earlier and said this was the best he's seen it."

The Gulch was exactly that, a monstrous ravine that ate neophyte skiers, and where large boulders terraced the fall. When covered with snow, these formed shoots that propelled undaunted skiers into flight. The fearless attempted helicopter-spins or eagle-spreads during the two-hundred-foot drop. Those who missed a turn survived on a castigating rear slide and a prayer of contrition. Mark preferred to consider it as it was in springtime, a tranquil waterfall by which to have a picnic.

"I think I'll pass it up, Victor," Emilia answered. "I had a bad spill on it last month… You were there when it happened."

"Yeah, but the snow was bad, too icy. Bob also took a spill then, worse than yours. He says now it's the best he's seen it. Come on, let's do it! There aren't any more storms in the forecast. It's the best it'll ever get."

"I'll pass it up, Victor. I don't want to spend the spring in crutches." As Victor controlled the conversation, Emilia alternated her glance between them.

History was communal but not necessarily universal. Mark could not think of a shared experience or any other way to join their conversation. He vigorously brushed at imaginary crumbs on his lap but surprised himself when he stood up. "I guess I better go," he said to cover for the disruption.

"Don't, Mark," she responded. "I didn't mean to ignore you."

"You didn't. I just have… some errands I need to get done." He committed to his rash decision.

"Will I see you tomorrow at breakfast?" she asked with a smile that relayed she enjoyed their brief time together.

He looked at Victor who was silently focused on Emilia. Mark wished more than crumbs on his lap. "Yes, I'll be there," he answered.

"Nice meeting you," added Victor, as if the last comment was required of him.

At the front of the lodge, Mark found Emilia's skis planted into the snow bank. He recognized them by their colors: turquoise banded the back, lavender on the front, and a stripe of gold parted them. These colors he recognized to be from the palette often preferred by Native American tribes in the Southwest.

He tuned into the music from the wind and continued in step to Emilia's dance. In its rhythm, he effortlessly skied down to the base lodge.

Chapter 6

From his rearview mirror, the ski runs appeared like white strips of decorative ribbons woven into the mountain; but he didn't care to look back for long: it reminded him of being in retreat. He tried to forget the impulse that made him walk away, but it only left him the image of Emilia's stare for him to stay. To forget was not to forgive because it hurt to imagine he had disappointed her once again.

◆ ◆ ◆

At the main traffic intersection back in town, he forced himself into a distraction by considering the Haiku poet and her fiancé's canned meal. As well, he was reminded of his empty cupboards.

A wide market aisle led him to the wine section, where he studied each bottle of Chardonnay by the thickness of its glass. Of the one chosen, he raised to eye-level and watched the refracted light become diffused into a spectrum of blush.

To cherished thoughts that kept our company, he remembered Belinda's rebuke to his gloom of dining alone. At that moment, he recalled Emilia's touch when he gripped the picnic table—he marched out of the market with an anticipation he had not recognized before.

◆◆◆

On passing the casino, Mark felt as if the car seemed to slow down of its own volition and turn back by an innate habit into the parking lot. Inside, the multicolored neon lights offered the only respite from the darkness. Looking about, he thought the casino appeared like an abstract garden, in which there had never been day. Among flowers that he knew would never bloom, a sparse crowd sat hunched over gaming tables and appeared to feast on melancholy. Like an elixir to their bewitched state, a clear yellow drink was set at hand's reach, and their attention was solely on the dealt cards before them. In the background, one-arm bandits loudly dropped silver coins into tin plates and preached a sermon to cajole gamblers to play further. On his rush out of the casino, Mark was greeted by a gentle breeze.

On the walk to his truck, he playfully jingled in his pocket the coins Emilia had given him for change. Amidst the trees covering the parking lot, there was no view of the mountains, but only of a luminous white ribbon he knew she would take on her last ski run.

From the deck of his home, he watched as dusk took a last peek above the rim of the mountains, and the sky became brushed with strokes of carbon. Gradually, clusters of stars flickered above him, and time became displayed in a monotone of colors.

Inside, he set the laptop on the dining table and felt his fingers gently stroke the keyboard. In dim light, so as not to dull the universe coming into view outside the window, he sat down to write.

From the *Incomplete Folder*, he reviewed his menagerie of characters, most of which had long ago been let to linger in a developing state. Of the female characters, he searched for one he could persuade to the spiritual comfort of a Native American tribe.

Though his characters were generally of European culture, he found Sadie, a mestiza woman of Mexican ancestry. With *cut and paste*, he clipped out Sadie from a band of hippies on a college break, traveling to the Santa Cruz Mountains for communal living, and posted her onto a unique *Word file* for further development.

Though he was anxious for Sadie's background to unfold further, he realized his lack of knowledge for the spiritual foundation from which Sadie's will and actions would be created. He looked out the window into a universe full of stars and excitedly recognized *hope*—which was eternal. He quickly shut the laptop off and proceeded to dream.

◆ ◆ ◆

He awakened into the active tense, in which he planned to write his characters. It was a cloudy morning, and a new crystalline lace of icicles clung from the railing, reminding him winter continued its struggle. He put on the ski jacket, expecting it would still be cold outside.

The road through town was quiet, and only two cars were parked in the lot at Maidu. With a blanket of ice clouding the cars' windows, he guessed they had been left overnight. He parked adjacent to the one closest to the entrance and wondered whether he had misjudged the time.

Discreetly, he snooped through the frosted side window of the adjacent vehicle, but it was not enough of a clear view to spy for items from Emilia's preferred palette. On suddenly hearing the café's front door being opened, he crouched and waited. No one came out, so he realized someone had entered. He rushed to get inside.

A gray-haired man sat at the counter with a newspaper held open in one hand, and a cup of coffee in the other. No one else was visible. He closed the door behind him as a waitress appeared from the kitchen.

He stood at the front, and as the waitress approached, she brushed away a smoke-gray curl that dangled over her forehead. Aside from the magenta on her lips and crow's feet sharpening the corners of her eyes, she appeared unremarkable. "Would you like a table?" she asked.

"No, thank you. I'll just eat at the counter." He continued to the second stool away from the gray-haired man, whose stare remained fixed on the paper. He heard nothing from the back of the café.

"G'morning," said the man, with a quick side-glance.

"Morning," Mark replied and skimmed the headlines of the business section the man was reading. "How's the world of money?"

"Good." His eyes did not waiver from the print. He set the cup on the saucer and turned the page to the stock prices. "I think the market's gettin' too pricey, though." He folded the paper and set it on the stool between them. "Laura, how about some more coffee?"

The woman wiped her hands on her apron as she returned from the kitchen. "I'm sorry, Warren. I'm by myself this mornin'. Just tryin' to catch up on some o' the preparations." From the back counter, she grabbed the coffee pot and approached the man. "How was breakfast?"

"Good," he answered, in the same tone with which he had reflected on the world of business.

"Havin' coffee this mornin'?" she asked Mark.

"Yes, please." He turned the cup over, and Laura poured the coffee as she steadily raised the pot. A pigmented froth appeared that quickened the steam and carried the aroma.

"Are you ready to order?"

"Didn't spill a drop... You are good!" he said. "Let me have a minute to look over the menu."

"I'll take the bill," Warren said and placed five dollars from his wallet on the check. "I gotta get goin'. Tell Emilia I missed her."

"Sure will. She'll open tomorrow." Laura pocketed the money and gathered the dishes, then returned into the kitchen.

Mark looked away from the menu to the front window. His vision felt as if blurred by the silence, but he stared beyond the window to the one parked car adjacent to his. As the sun had scaled the mountain rim, the sheet of ice on the windshield began to drip into beads of water. Remorse overwhelmed him as he thought Emilia was probably with Victor.

"Have you made up your mind?" Laura asked from the kitchen door.

"I'll have an egg bagel sandwich." He did not look away from the window and no longer felt hungry.

It wasn't long before Laura returned with the sandwich; but in his trance of regrets, time was not a factor.

"Everything okay?" Laura asked and refilled the cup.

"Yeah, I think so." He turned back to the meal and raised his arms behind his head as if to hold back his thoughts. "You didn't pour from up high this time."

"I didn't think you were payin' attention... You seem out of it."

"It's too early in the morning. I'm just tired," he said

and reached for the newspaper.

"Tell me about it. I switched shifts today, so I had to open." Laura wiped the counter where Warren had eaten. "Honey, it's sure hard to wake up when it's darker outside than when you went to sleep." She returned to the kitchen.

He was glad no response was required and, instead, reached for the business section Warren had left. The first article predicted an inevitable market correction; but equally convincing was a second pundit in a later segment discussing the economic parameters that would maintain the bull market.

What higher value had an expert's opinion than a rabbit's foot? he thought of the discussions in the business section. Their odds were those of Trapper Garza, *Whichever way they turn.* Though *to forget did not forgive,* he was grateful for the distraction.

Mark took the bill to the cash register and waited for Laura. He had not noticed the two diners arrive at the table by the window. Beyond them outside, the car next to his remained unmoved, but its ice covering had fully melted.

Laura took the money. "How was breakfast?" she asked but did not look up from the cash drawer.

"Good." He mimicked Warren's assessment to pretend nonchalance. At the counter, he left two dollars. "Is Emilia working later today?"

"She better get here soon. People are startin' to come in," Laura replied, then crossed the room to the new diners.

He zipped the jacket and tucked his hands deep into its pockets to thwart the cold. Behind him, the screen door clapped shut as he put on his gloves. The view into the first car was no longer smeared by ice, but he stooped instead towards the door of his truck. With gloved hands, he fumbled with the keys.

An older model car drove up to the front of the coffee shop. Mark gazed through the window of his door and saw Emilia step out from the passenger side. She bent down to the side-window and continued a conversation with the driver. A concluding chuckle was all Mark could understand.

Inconspicuously, he crouched to below the level of the roof of his truck and canvassed the car when it drove by. An androgynous silhouette of the driver was all he managed to discern.

"Mark?" Emilia called from the café entrance. "Is that you?"

The keys dropped from his hand and clinked on the gravel. He straightened as if commanded. "Hi." He cleared his throat.

"Coming in for breakfast?" She leaned to the jamb and held the screen door partly open; the indoor light shadowed her smile.

"I just finished." He bit his lower lip, but could not think of how to withdraw the comment. *Was it a sickness he was catching?*

"You got here earlier than usual, but then I'm late." She opened the door wider and motioned toward the inside. Her smile faded. "I better go. Laura is probably upset."

As soon as the door closed behind her, she reopened it. "I'm meeting some friends at Steamers tonight, about seven. I would like it if you could come," she said.

Emilia recognized the gleam from his smile as assent and let the door clap shut behind her.

Chapter 7

A sundial marks time by the drift of shadows, yet Mark felt time by the dispersion of warmth across his forehead. Bent over his laptop and concentrated on his research, it was the cool of evening that roused him.

Writing fiction was his binary entertainment: imprinted digitally and without consequence. He straightened in his chair and saved the burgeoning file for Sadie into the *Incomplete Folder*. It had been an arduous job: every word he incorporated in developing Sadie's background had required to be researched.

Fate he was determined to make a primary theme for Sadie's story. *It is the sum of personal turns of events, with divinity its ultimate source.* He glanced away from reading the lines he had written and was reminded of his abdominal scar: the result of stepping away from the order Sadie would follow.

Excitedly, he prepared to meet Emilia at Steamers and became committed to doing as Trapper Garza had advised: to let it happen *whichever way it turned*.

◆◆◆

Only a few cars were parked outside the restaurant. Mark quickly scanned for the older model Emilia had gotten out of earlier that morning. Glad on noticing it absent, he let the androgynous form of the driver remain a mental silhouette.

At the entryway to Steamer's, Mark brushed the flat tops of his sneakers again; but failing to muster a shine, he continued into the foyer.

"Table for one?" greeted the hostess.

"No," he replied almost defensively. "I'm waiting for some people."

"Maybe they're already here. What party are you with?" She turned to scout the almost empty dining area.

He creased the pleats of his pants, embarrassed at not knowing what name to ask for. He stared away from the hostess to the lounge. "I don't think they've arrived yet," he said.

"You can wait for them in there," she said pointing to the lounge, "or here," and walked him to a wooden chair at a corner of the foyer. She returned to behind the podium and resumed her paperwork.

From the wooden chair, he looked over to the dim lounge, where a lone bartender washed drinking glasses that he hung on an overhead track at the bar. A muted sound of disco music floated from the room.

Lighting in the dining area was likewise dim. Large upholstered chairs engulfed the few diners who sat on them. *Whispers*, Mark thought, would make a better name than *Steamers*, as it was all he could make out from their conversations.

Sitting alone in the corner of the foyer, he began to feel conspicuous, as the lint on his blue woolen sweater gradually became. His only distraction was to pick at the fuzz.

Two couples, chattering jovially, entered from the front and proceeded to the lounge. Mark recognized

Laura, the Maidu waitress, but lacking an introduction, he was hesitant to approach the group. Instead, he left the restaurant for a short walk.

There was not much of the town's commercial area to wander through, but he felt it an endless journey for the many thoughts that crossed his mind encouraging him to return home. It was the memory of Emilia's eyes requesting he not leave that compelled him to return.

"You're here," the hostess said when he re-entered the foyer. "What party were you waiting for?"

There were many more diners in the restaurant, and Emilia had joined the earlier group still in the lounge.

"I see them," he responded. "Thanks."

Emilia sat at a table facing the entrance, but was distracted in spirited conversation with two couples. Mark recognized the ski-lodge café attendant seated beside her. He decided to sit at the first table he came upon but pulled the chair into the shadows.

Mark shut his eyes to entrench his isolation and recalled the smile of her victorious hoot over the moguls. Deep in imagery, he let his body sway to the soft rock music that filled the lounge as if he was in dance on the moguls.

"Falling asleep?"

Startled that his imagination could be so vivid, he opened his eyes and quickly straightened in the chair. Emilia stood across from him.

"Oh—gee—no," he stammered. "I was just thinking—I'm sorry. I didn't mean to take you away from your friends."

"I was afraid you wouldn't join us. Besides, I see them almost every day." She rested her hand on top of the opposite chair. "Would you mind?"

"Oh, please do," he said and rushed to the chair she

held. He hesitated to draw it out. "If you rather, we can go over to your friends."

"Let's just sit here for a while," she said, and Mark pulled out the chair for her to sit.

"I was working up the courage to go over to your friends," he said. "But I like this much better."

"There's no need for courage… You know Laura from Maidu?" Emilia turned to better point out her friends, who continued in animated conversation. "John, next to her, is her husband. He's a delivery guy in town. Bob, you may have seen, is ski patrol, and Barbara is his most recent girlfriend. She's a receptionist at the Hyatt. Norma you met at the lodge, remember?"

Mark casually listened, fixated on her facial features that seemed to reveal an intimacy for each of her introductions. He quickly looked away toward her friends when she turned to him.

"Yes," he answered, wondering whether Bob was Victor's twin. "I'm no longer intimidated—we don't have to stay in the shadows if you don't want."

"I'm glad we're alone," she replied.

He felt her words enclose them as if into a cocoon. Mark returned her gaze: she was all he cared to know about, *and I got's all the time in the world to know here well,* he recalled Trapper Garza mention.

"Are they all friends?" he asked.

"Yes, except for Barbara. I just met her tonight. The others I've known since I moved to Tahoe." Her fingers gently touched the cardboard doily on the table. Her glance remained on him.

"Let me get you something from the bar," he suggested. "Chardonnay?"

"That would be nice."

Mark crossed the lounge to the bar, feeling

enchanted in the spotlight of her gaze. The overhead lights seemed dim in comparison. On the return, he cradled the bottle in the crook of his left arm and, with the lightest touch, gripped the stem of two crystal glasses. On the polished dance floor, he shuffled to the music as he returned, as a moth would to a lantern.

"Now if I only had some candles," he said and placed the glass before her, "the mood would be picture-perfect."

"Maybe if we were working on a greeting card," she responded. "Otherwise, I'm more inclined to let whatever happen."

"I'm sure you're right, but I've been out of the scene for a while and need some props, at least 'til I get some confidence." Mark poured the wine into each of their glasses and sat onto his chair.

"Props are good," she said and looked at him with a smile. "We could all use reassurance."

"Let me make a toast."

"Please do." She raised her glass to meet his, and, refracted through the crystal, the light of the room sprinkled across the table at the turn of her glass.

"To romance and spring snow!" he said.

"It sounds like something from a poem," she added.

"It's just an off-the-cuff salutation you inspired."

"Is there meaning to it, besides being a prop?" she asked.

"Ah, let's see. How about: 'as with winter, so with romance, each adversity heralds a springtime bloom.'" Mark raised one eyebrow and grimaced in anticipation of her response.

There was a pause, during which she appeared pensive. "I think there's poetic potential there."

"I'll work on it," he offered and took a second drink.

He glanced through the crystal at her smile. "Where are you originally from?" he asked and leaned forward.

"From Georgia." She held the glass to her lips.

"A Georgia peach!" he embellished.

"Without the fuzz," she interjected. "I'm just a simple Cherokee."

"So that's why Norma said you go to Berkeley for prayers with Native Americans."

"You don't have to be Native American for prayers." She sipped at the wine, and a drop spilled onto her chin.

Mark handed her a napkin across the table and she dabbed it dry. "Oh, I know," he said, "but I'd wondered about it when Norma mentioned it at the lodge." He leaned back on the chair. "You may think badly of me, but I don't know much about the history of the Indians—I mean, Native Americans—even though I write a magazine column based on the history of the Old West."

"Don't worry about it. People satisfy only their interests." Emilia leaned forward with her fingers encircling the base of the glass set on the table. "You're not local, are you?"

"A native Californian," he answered, glad for the change in subject. "A direct descendant of a Spanish Conquistador." Mark felt a cool sweat form at the back of his neck when he realized their discordant ancestry. He looked to the darkness that enclosed the dance floor and, as if to the screen of a confessional, blurted out, "I'm sure he was just a journalist, keeping an account of their adventures. That's where I got my writing talent, you know."

Her chuckle welcomed him back from his presumption. "If we had to answer for our fathers' sins," she said, "the earth would indeed be hell."

The music was livelier than when he had crossed the dance floor, and more conversation was audible from other tables around them. Mark also noticed two others had joined Emilia's friends, and he was glad her back was turned to them: Victor had joined the group.

In an effort to lock her attention, Mark quickly added, "Tahoe is where I feel most at home... My paradise."

"Lake Tahoe is definitely a corner of heaven."

"What brought you here from Georgia?" he asked.

"I wanted to take time off after college and experience some of the things I had read about." She sipped the wine and paused. "I've spent time in other parts of the country, but I felt a spiritualism here that is... magnetic."

"I think I know what you mean, but I've never put it in those terms."

"Actually, I don't know why I've stayed. It's like my senses created a tempo that now simply directs my life."

Her introspective stare that followed seemed as in search beyond the confines of the room, and he wanted to pull her back. "What did you study in college?"

"Religious studies." She returned her gaze to Mark.

"Really?" He restrained the surprise in his inflection. "What are you doing as a waitress?"

"What does anyone do with work but pay for a livelihood."

"I mean, shouldn't you be working in a church, or some job requiring a ministry?" He smiled to reveal the intended humor. "I mean, judging a guy who drips egg yolk on his shirt doesn't require a degree... Maybe it does... What do I know?"

"I wanted the historical perspective." Her hazel eyes held a distant but delighted gaze. "I figured life could be more fulfilling and engaging if I knew how and why things came to be." Emilia brushed back an unruly curl. "Actually, being a waitress has been quite good." She leaned forward, her elbows on the table, and rested her chin on the back of her folded hands. "Think of all the rewards—dripping yolk and all the breakfast gore."

He wanted to feel the soft flesh of her face and twine the curl of her hair between his fingers. There were a million thoughts he wanted to share. Instead, he laughed.

"And what's *your* reason?" she asked.

"I'm sorry—my reason for what?"

"Why are you in Lake Tahoe?"

"Wait a minute. We weren't finished with *your* story." The music sounded louder with a beat that prodded him to stand. "Would you like to dance?"

"I'd love to!"

He held her hand and led to the center of the empty dance floor. Mark recognized Gordon Lightfoot's *Early Morning Rain*. A bit hillbilly, he thought, but the tune was infectious. He watched Emilia prance about with a country western foot movement popular in northern Nevada. After tripping a few times clumsily, he abandoned his attempt to mimic her steps.

The curls of her hair danced on her shoulders; each brunette fiber was silhouetted against the ceiling lights. Her rouged lips, thinly parted, formed a smile that highlighted the whiteness of her teeth. The coral rose of her cardigan flattered her skin, and its embroidery broadened the fullness of her breasts. Turquoise trousers hung from her slim waist, contouring the curve of her hips. The trouser legs fitted snugly into the tops of worn leather boots. Mark thought Emilia was more than the Maidu oracle—she was a Cherokee princess. To the whirlwind of sound, she pirouetted on the axis of her body. Mark was drawn in by the contagion of her joy. He reached for her outstretched hand.

The music slowed to Chris Isaak's *Two Hearts*. Mark raised their clasped hands and drew her near. With one arm around her waist, he guided her movement, and together they glided across the wooden floor. Her legs brushed the inside of his at each of their turns.

Emilia swayed gently to *When I Fall in Love* by Rick Astley and pressed her body to his. Mark felt the moisture of her hand when it slipped away to embrace him. She rested her head in the cradle of his shoulder. Silk, he imagined, was no softer than the feel of her hair against his cheek. He then only thought of writing her a poem:

> *Caterpillars spin into a shelter of delicate fibers*
> *and dance in circles of an impassioned universe.*
> *Closed eyes see desire;*
> *in these shadows is a different world.*
> *In which they are the earth and the moon,*
> *intertwined in an embrace.*

The melody shifted to rock 'n' roll, and their trance was disrupted. Three couples took to the dance floor and displaced them. He held her hand when they returned to the table.

From her purse, she withdrew a tissue and wiped the beads of sweat on her forehead. "Would you like one?"

He smelled her fragrance on him. "I'm fine. Thanks."

"You dance well," she said and sat down.

"I'm only as good as my partner." Mark hesitated to sit and watched as Emilia's friends entered the dance floor. He noticed Victor appeared to whisper into Norma's ear and nod in their direction.

"I'm sorry I missed you at breakfast today," she said, "but I'm very glad you came tonight. I was afraid you wouldn't."

"It was all I could think of," he replied and hurried to his chair, hoping to keep her turned away from the dancers. "Breakfast was not as good as usual," and, without taking a breath, added, "Do you come here often?"

Emilia turned to the finger tapping her shoulder. "Norma!" she said and glanced to her friends across the room. "Looks like you guys are having a good time… Norma, this is Mark."

With a slight turn to Mark, Norma replied, "Hi." But without a pause, she returned to Emilia. "Come back and join us? Victor is here."

Mark noticed Emilia's slight sneer in response but then smiled when she asked him, "Would you like to join them?"

No, he thought would be selfish, and *yes* a lie. "You go ahead. I have work to do, anyway." He dropped back into his chair.

"Work is an overused excuse." She touched his hand clutching the edge of the table. "I want you to stay."

As if there was magic in her touch, he felt himself with butterfly wings unfurl from a cocoon. His smile stretched every wrinkle on his face. "You're right, time to bury old excuses."

He refilled his wine glass and reminded himself *in life there is never a guarantee;* but what he wished for was a reassurance, and that came with her touch when she led him across the dance floor.

Joining the group, Mark and Emilia danced to a tune that mocked their earlier passion: frivolous body movements foiled his attempt at pair dancing. While Laura tightly grasped her husband John, Bob seductively glanced at Barbara, as Emilia and Norma twirled among Victor, Ray, and Mark.

After a non-stop session of dancing, Mark was first to tire and withdraw to the table that served as the group's base, a trestle for their drinks. Leaning forward on the chair, he stared beyond the empty wine bottle to where Emilia remained prancing to the music.

"Well, old man, did you get your fill?" Ray punctuated his question with a slap to Mark's back as he accompanied Norma to the table. Ray was a local contractor and father of three but was separated from his wife. He had arrived earlier with Victor.

"I think I did," Mark replied, "but you don't look in any better shape."

Bob and Barbara joined them at the table but stood to the side, where the light was most dim. He kissed her on the lips and then bent his head to lick the sweat from her neck.

Laura sat at the table and wiped her face with a handkerchief. John searched the bottles and, on a single gulp, emptied the one left with beer. Though both were middle-aged, Mark gauged them to be older than himself.

"Bob seems a bit thirsty," John said about the couple still locked in a kiss. "I think he would do better to drink some beer."

"I don't know about that, John," said Ray with a glance to Norma. "I wouldn't mind some of what he's getting."

"If you ask me, you're getting too much of it outside

your own home," Laura interjected.

"Ouch, Laura!" Ray replied with folded hands gripped tight between his thighs. "It's been a while since I've had any, though… I've done my penance, and I'm sure Marge will take me back. She knows everything else meant nothing."

"She's a good woman. I think she'll forgive you," added Norma, staring at Emilia and Victor on the dance floor. "Don't they make a good couple?"

The conversation had been like lint on his sweater, a good distraction from Emilia and Victor on the dance floor; but Norma's observation shattered the screen. Mark looked up and could not help but agree: they did appear a good couple.

Before the music had finished, Emilia walked toward their table. Victor followed two feet behind her, his arms reaching as if to catch up. He leaned to her and whispered, but Mark could only look away.

With a swift brush of Mark's hair, Emilia nudged him to move his chair and took the adjacent seat. From his glass, she sipped from the wine that remained.

Mark stared at the impression of her lipstick left on the rim of the crystal as he reached for the glass. Furtively, he ran his finger along the edge of the imprint.

When the music reached a louder pitch, Laura tugged at John's hand and motioned toward the front door. Bob placed a jacket over Barbara's shoulders and embraced her from behind. Norma searched in her purse and retrieved a silver ring from which hung a million keys. Ray stood away from the table and jingled coins in his pants pocket. Victor sat deep in his chair staring calmly at Emilia, who tightened the belt of her overcoat.

"Would you like a ride home?" Victor asked her.

"I'm going back with Norma. Thanks," she replied

and glanced at Mark, who had quietly stepped away from the group.

At the foyer, each in the group bade the other goodnight. Emilia stepped back to where Mark had lagged.

"I had a very good time," she said and cupped his chin in her hand to lower for a kiss.

"I'm glad I stayed," he replied and licked his lips.

At the parking lot, Emilia rejoined the group, and Mark heartily smiled on noticing her enter the old model car, in which Norma waited in the driver's seat.

On the sound of crinkled paper, he opened his hand. As if to reveal a treasured map, he unraveled the wrinkled edges: a note on which Emilia had written her telephone number.

Warmed in his wool jacket, he stood on the cold asphalt and again licked his lip for the taste of Emilia.

Chapter 8

On the coast from San Jose, monarch butterflies migrate north in spring to return later in the fall, traveling hundreds of miles on their journey. *Nature is patient,* he reminded himself, to calm the restlessness that kept him up much of that night. In tossing and turning, he often sought for a hint of daylight through the open blinds of his bedroom.

On his step out of bed he heard paper crinkle and reached to find Emilia's note, fallen from the nightstand. "Call me tomorrow," he read. The flourishes in her handwriting bespoke her invitation.

Mark returned the note to the table but hoisted it for prominent display over a pyramid of coins. *It's too early to call,* he cautioned himself. *She would still be at work.*

Outside the shower, he struggled with the towel around his waist, as droplets dripped from his hair on each glance to the mirror—and the reflection of the phone. *It's still too early to call.*

Minutes on the clock were counted slower, so he thought it best to leave time unattended—it would pass more swiftly. He went on a tour of the neighborhood.

A red-tail hawk flew over the road and into the forest that Mark rarely visited. Its distant squall sounded like a poetic recital, carrying a rhythm he knew belonged to the forest. It was poetry he hoped Emilia would enjoy.

Back inside his home, he remembered Emilia's recognition of his toast's poetic potential and decided to work on her poem. He hoped to offer it as a serenade.

With repetition comes memory, and it is what became of her telephone number after he had frequently read her note. Dialing it was an unconscious act, but the male voice that took the call rang out like thunder—Mark hung up in reflex. To redial, he carefully matched each number to those on her note, but the same monotone voice answered. To defy the voice's request to leave a message, he slammed down the phone.

It was a long while before he reclaimed the courage to redial her number. "Hello?" answered a female voice.

"Hi, Emilia?" he asked but did not recognize the voice.

"No, but just a minute. I'll get her."

"Hi... Mark?" Emilia asked.

"How did you know it was me?"

"I'm the Maidu Oracle, remember? Actually, Laura thought it was you." There was a brief conversation away from the phone until she continued, "We just got in from grocery shopping."

"I'll call later if you want. I'm sure you're busy."

"No, no. Laura is on her way out. She just ran in to use the bathroom." He heard Emilia tell Laura to call later, and then return to the line. "I'm sorry. It gets hectic on shopping days. I try not to do it too often, but I suppose I have to eat."

"Maybe I could be of help with that and cook dinner for you one day." Mark lay back on the bed, a rolled pillow propped beneath his head. "It might save you on shopping time."

"Well, that would certainly be nice," she replied.

He heard the sound of cans into cabinets. "You're not vegetarian, are you?" he asked.

"Oh, no. But I'll only eat what Walt Disney has not made a movie of." They laughed.

"I guess I better get to a video store," he added, "to make a safe shopping list."

"Let's watch 'Bambi' after dinner," she suggested.

"Anything you want. I'll make it your day."

"I'll hold you to it," she said.

"I'm sure my cooking will impress you."

"At least we won't have much cleaning to do," she mocked. "You sure leave those breakfast dishes clean. A dog would starve waiting for your leftovers."

"I'm getting self-conscious here. Do I eat that poorly?"

"I'm only kidding." There was a pause during which he heard her sigh. "I've enjoyed watching you eat… For the last two years, it's all you've shared with me."

He let the weight of her words push him deeper onto the bed. *One dwells in solitude*, he thought, *but is not engaged by it.*

Her distant voice came from the handset that had slipped from his ear, "Hello? Mark?"

"I'm sorry. I dropped the phone." He hesitated, then added, "All the more reason to have you over for dinner. There's no excuse but tunnel vision to have ignored you."

"There's no need for an excuse," she replied. "But I would love to take you up on dinner."

"When?" he asked.

"Not today. Laura and I ate all the unwrapped items we bought at the market, and now I'm stuffed."

"Today is only Tuesday. Let's make it Friday," he said.

"It's a date." After a pause, she added, "It's so beautiful outside, and I really need to walk off some of the food I ate. Would you like to join me on a hike in the forest?"

Outside his window, the mound of snow on his deck continued to drip in a stream of water; a thin layer of mist above it splayed the sunlight into a rainbow of colors. It was springtime, and he wanted to listen to the poetic recital in the forest. "I'd love to," he responded.

◆◆◆

Heavy snow seemed to have isolated the heavily wooded peninsula. Where the park jutted into the lake at the southern end of town, granite boulders formed a rampart at the water's edge.

Double tire marks tracked through the frozen snow into the park. He maneuvered the truck along them to the solitary jeep parked in a grotto of evergreens.

In the wintry seclusion, snow still blanketed the summer trails, and tall drifts lingered in the shadows of the redwoods. Like arrows of light, beams of sun flashed through the canopy to patiently thin the snow.

"You made it here quickly," Emilia welcomed him from the trail that led away from the snow-covered lot. She held gloves in one hand and, with the other, waved Mark to follow. He recognized the green ski jacket she wore with a blue nylon leg-shell strapped to the collars of leather snow boots and covering her trousers.

"It's cold out here," he said and walked to where she stood.

"I suppose you weren't expecting much snow." He followed her glance at what he wore: his hands were bare beyond the cuff of the knitted sweater, which hung loosely over his corduroy slacks.

He shivered at a cold gust of wind. "Maybe I should get my jacket." He ran back to his truck.

"We'll stay around the beach," she suggested and started on the trail. "The snow has pretty much melted there."

The trail had been manually hewn out of knee-deep frozen snow and wended its way through a stretch of forest. The muffled sound of their step on frozen ground blended with the streaming of melting snow. The percussion of a woodpecker kept their pace from above them, and, like melodious notes, footprints of deer trailed in between the trees.

"Do you think we'll see Bambi?" Mark asked.

She laughed. "I was just thinking the same thing!"

The dense forest opened to an expansive panorama of the lake. From the shoreline, turquoise waters seemed to unfurl to a royal blue at the center of the lake. The surrounding mountains, contrasted by the cloudless sky, were reflected on the water.

Gentle waves lapped at the pebble beach on which the trail had led them, but it was the warming from the afternoon sun he most appreciated. He shuddered with the chill of his feet. "Oh my. I got my socks all soaked." He motioned his step to re-create the squish inside the sneakers.

"It might be better if you take your shoes and socks off," Emilia said. "I think it's warm enough for them to dry."

Embarrassed, Mark did as she suggested and rolled the legs of his pants to his knees. He relished the warm feel of the sun on his wet feet.

Gripping the sneakers at their collar, with the socks loosely hanging from inside, he stood ready to march on. "All right, I think this'll work," he said.

They continued on the trail until it ended at the granite face of behemoth boulders that were banked one upon the other. These appeared as if in a timeless promenade to the lake.

Emilia stopped, with the crest of the rampart well above her head. A gentle wind fluffed her hair as she gauged the best route to take.

On the beach, where it felt warmest, a few feet from where she searched, Mark laid out his shoes and socks to dry.

"Mark, come up here," she called from atop the last boulder to the lake, several feet above the water. "It's nice and warm up here." Her face was illuminated by direct sunlight; her hair was blown back at the temples.

From where he stood on the beach, the rampart's facade seemed vertical to its summit. Toward the lake, the pebbled beach sank into the frigid water. Beyond the beach, into the forest, deep snow filled the shaded precipice. There seemed no option: Mark confronted the rock wall, as he thought she must have done. Her shadow above him tendered a dare, but he did not ask her for direction.

Upside against the rocky wall, he groped for a secure handhold and found a small promontory that jutted out at the level of his hip. He jammed the toes of one foot onto it and lifted himself. With one hand, he reached a crevice at arm's length above his head, and his body became flushed against the rock. The fall below and the climb ahead were equidistant. He became committed to reaching her side.

On the craggy surface of a second foothold, he managed to heave his body's weight and reach with his hand the crest that loomed above his head. Stretching both arms, he gripped the rocky cornice above him, but

Alvarado

his foot slipped from its toehold. The right knee scraped the rock as he hung suspended from the capstone. He dug his fingers into the granite and, with a burst of strength, lifted himself onto the ledge.

"Are you all right?" Emilia asked on hearing his groan. "It would've been easier around this end."

He turned away from the view of the fall he would have taken to the stepping-stone approach where she pointed.

"My way was more… adventurous," he gasped.

When Emilia turned away toward the lake, he quickly rolled the leg of his pants to inspect the trickle of blood he felt on the right knee. Assessing it a minor wound, he unraveled the pants leg to conceal the injury.

"Is it nature or nurture?" she asked.

He sat next to her and stared into the lake, to where he thought her focus was. He worked on nonchalance before he replied, "What do you mean?"

"Why are men like boys?" she asked. "There always has to be some personal challenge in everything."

The warm moisture at his knee felt as if it was spreading. He pressed his hand more firmly against the wound and mimicked her laughter. "Would you rather it one way over the other?" he asked.

"I like it the way it is." She turned to look at him. A strengthened breeze fanned a strand of hair across her face and stole away her gaze. Gently, she brushed back the wanton curls. "But in fact, nature is our nurture," she said as if to answer her thoughts. "I look at everything here—the boulder we sit on, the lake so deep, the mountain that changes colors with the weather—and I wonder whether we are like everything else: become only what is destined?"

"Is that what you referred to last night?" he asked. "I

mean, about this place having magnetic spiritualism?"

"That's just where to begin." She looked at the water and her reflection. A curl dropped to her forehead and she brushed it back. "I feel as beautiful as everything else around me."

"You are beautiful."

"And that is what I mean: nature is our nurture. Your thinking I am beautiful makes you want more." She glanced at him and asked, "So, do you think we make our destiny, or do we become what we are destined?"

"Which one do you think?"

"A question is never an answer." Emilia turned her body to him. With her knees flexed, she wrapped her arms around her legs. "Which would make you happiest?"

"My catechism nun never asked these questions." He looked away. "Are these propositions you go to Berkeley to pray for, or simply inquiries for your religious studies?"

"I don't know." She hesitated with a sigh and brushed back a wave of his hair that undulated over his forehead with the breeze. "I did pray to be here with you."

"Why?... Because I drip egg yolk on my shirt?"

"Yes," she answered and looked into his eyes.

"Oh, so you prefer the clumsy type." He looked away to cover up not understanding but noticed the red halo appearing to have enlarged on his right knee. He pressed harder to stop the blood flow. As if compelled by an impulse, he quickly rose and ran the stepping stones into the lake.

"Mark, where are you going?" she called from behind him.

"Into these spiritual waters!" To mock old-time

prayer revivals, he flapped his hands above his head and walked into the frigid water. "I will not be destined to eternal clumsiness!"

"Come out of there!" she yelled to him from where the water lapped at her feet. "I promise I won't talk in allegories!"

He waited for the trickle of blood to be halted by the cold water, and for the red stain at his knee to be cleansed. "It's not your allegories I don't understand," he said as he lumbered from the waist-deep water. "I just don't want to disappoint you."

Emilia smiled and wrapped her arms around his neck when he came to the water's edge. "The opportunity to be disappointed is the chance for love," she said.

Raised to her tiptoes, he firmly embraced her for a kiss. She slipped her hands to his chest and gently pushed away.

"We better get you dry and warmed up," she said. His lips quivered with the muscles of his jaw as she scanned him from head to toe. "I only live a mile down the road."

The wet pants clung to him and dripped water from the unraveled cuffs. His toes were blanched, but he walked onto the beach without hesitation. His socks were almost dry, but water seeped through the canvas when he forced the sneakers back on.

"I'm ready. Lead me to your home," he commanded, with an impish smile frozen on his face.

Chapter 9

It was difficult to walk with the sneakers squishing and pants swishing on every step he took. Most difficult was to sprint on a stiff knee, but Mark managed to keep close to her pace going out of the park. He felt his smile, as if it was frozen, when he returned to the parking lot.

"Follow me," she shouted getting into her truck.

Once inside his truck, Mark set the heater at full blast. With the vent directed to his feet, he wiggled his toes still inside the shoes, afraid they would not fit once removed. With his heel pressed to the accelerator, he hoped there would not be much pain when his toes would begin to thaw.

Going south, Mark followed Emilia away from town and up a hill into a thicker forest. Soiled snow bordered the road as the lake was lost among interpolated stalks of redwood pine.

In the early evening, the deep green canopy of the forest appeared as if sketched against the indigo blue at the skyline. To the west, the sunset waned into bands of golden clouds, woven with strings of lavender. Inspired by the celestial canvas, he worked on more poetic prose: *Words are like the colors of passion, and I'll make these the watercolors for her poem.*

As if in a trance, he retraced the feel of her kiss with a lick of his lips and, to reimagine the warmth of her breath, he turned a vent to flush his face. At the point she made a turn, the sudden flash of her brake lights forced him to a screeching stop.

"Ouch! Damn it!" he said to the pain of half-thawed toes.

The side road they took led further into the forest. Past granite outcrops, they drove into a narrow valley where the gravel road continued to a small rock-faced house. Its mallard-green roof was partly camouflaged under the overhang of the forest, and vaults of snow still clung to its eaves.

Mark parked at a walkway, carved into hardened snow, that led to the front door.

Like an inverted crystalline pyramid, a wind chime hung frozen within an icicle, drops of water its only melody. Emilia waited at the door. "Welcome to Hansel and Gretel's cabin!"

He walked stiffly to silence his clothing. "You must be Gretel," he said from inside the door. "I hope Hansel is out at play with the three bears."

"You've confused the fairy tales. But no, Hansel is up there." Emilia pointed to a large mohair effigy of Bullwinkle that hung over the fireplace mantle in the front corner of the living room. Its head was crowned with a Georgia Tech cap. "He's pretty good company, particularly on long winter nights."

"So, if you were to replace me for company, is that where you would place me as well?" Mark approached the mantle but sidestepped the Middle Eastern rug on the wooden floor. "I know someone who might look good affixed to that mantle, though."

In the center of the small room, Emilia sat on a love

seat that faced the cold hearth. She draped the jacket over the armrest. "Who would that be?"

"What's that guy's name?" He feigned indignation.

She stood up to the bar table on the opposite wall that separated the living room from a tidy kitchen and set her car keys on the counter. "What guy is that?"

"That guy who tried to take you home last night."

Filtered sunlight from a small window on the third wall dimly illuminated the room. Emilia walked to a side table at the far end of the sofa and turned on a Tiffany replica of a Dragonfly lamp. He felt his shadow thrown to the wall and expected a slap.

"Mark, you're not serious!" The polychrome glow from the lampshade shadowed her face. "He's just a good friend."

"I'm sorry if I misjudged," he replied and hesitated before adding, "but there was more than friendship in his eyes."

"Well, I won't argue that. He does have the cutest bedroom eyes." A slap would have been less painful than the abrupt end to the discussion.

From ceiling to floor, shelves laden with books lined the fourth wall. Adjacent to the book cabinet was an opened door, through which Emilia exited. A light was switched on where she entered, and Mark heard the zap of a zipper.

"Make yourself comfortable," she called back to him.

Like the ripple of moonlight on lake water, the light from her room was scattered over the seams of the floorboards. Mark remained at the edge of the rug, feeling the stiffness of his wet pants.

"This is a nice house," he said as he approached the open door.

"I love it here. It used to be the home of the

groundskeeper for a wealthy estate." She returned to the living room wearing a thin cotton pullover sweater, draped loosely to the hips of snug-fitting blue jeans. Her feet appeared warm in woolen socks. "The main house at the lakefront burned down in the 60s, and all the property was given up to the National Park Service. Now I rent this cabin from them."

"How did you find it?"

"Victor found it for me. You know—that guy with the bedroom eyes you would like hung over the mantle." From a wicker scuttle, Emilia grabbed two split wood logs and knelt by the fireplace. She looked up at Mark. "You don't have to stand there. Have a seat."

"My pants are still wet."

"Well, for God's sake, take them off."

Emilia's recommendation carried a tone that startled Mark, but he remained still to watch her gather splinters of wood from the scuttle and set a match to its hand-fisted mound. Fixated on a thin stream of smoke that rose in a spiral from the fledgling fire into the flue, they remained silent.

When the fire was well-established, he stepped away into her bedroom and removed the stiff clothing. To pull off the shoes and socks, he sat on the floor, but the feel of the cold wood against his buttocks did not stun him as the scream that followed.

"Mark!" she shouted from the fireplace. "You cut your knee!"

"It's fine." In reflex, he placed his hand firmly over the wound as if to conceal it. "It'll heal without any bother. The lake water cleaned it well."

"You've been hiding it since then?"

Emilia dropped the logs over the mound of splinters and scooted over to Mark and inspected the wound.

"It looks like it needs stitches." She looked up at him. "We better go to a doctor."

"It's okay." He forced confidence into his voice.

"It must be hard being a man," she said. "What would it take to make you cry?" She probed the wound with her fingers to calculate how wide the gap would open and determined that the edges came together at an even plane.

"Ai!" he said faintly. With gritted teeth and mist in his eyes, he then added, "How about some Cherokee shaman healing prayers instead?"

"Don't have much experience with that," Emilia replied. "When I was seven, though, I did watch my grandmother deliver a neighbor's child... I'll just pretend to be a nurse, as I did then."

With a glance up from the gash, she expressed an impish smile, upon which Mark would rather place his trust than on going to a doctor. He held back from touching her hand while she explored the wound. "What have you got there?" he asked.

"Go take a shower and clean the wound with this soap." She handed him an antiseptic solution, along with a towel and bathrobe. "Make sure you clean it well."

The shirttail draped over his briefs on the way to the bathroom. He planned on a cold shower to chill the excitement he feared was obvious. On the gush of the cold spray, he worked on distracting his attention: a method he often applied to fend off the pain. He sniffed two bottles of the hair products inside a metal basket that hung from the shower spout and recognized their scent as that of her hair. He read their labels as an anthropologist does hieroglyphics: a jojoba conditioner promised a desert star's sheen, and the mango conditioner the gloss of tropical rain.

Like camellia petals in bloom, the fabric scrub appeared flared open on the porcelain basin. He reached for it and lathered up the soap she had handed him. Only her shower cap fitted awkwardly.

A rose-colored froth foamed from his wound when he brushed at the knee and trickled down his leg to swirl into the drain. *Damn it! I stirred up the bleeding!* he mentally shouted.

With pressure applied with a washcloth, he managed to stop the ooze of blood. Contriving a bandage from the washcloth, he felt assured blood would not stain the cotton bathrobe Emilia had handed him: a man's robe with the smell of a recent wash. "Emilia!" he called out from her room. "Don't you think last night Victor had an ulterior motive?"

"What?" Her voice returned.

He sat on the corner of her bed and carefully looked over the robe he wore. Familiarity, he thought before replying, is the reward from intimacy; it cannot be simply granted from a stolen sniff of her shampoo. He asked anyway, "Whose bathrobe?"

"I don't know." Emilia's tone was that of a tease. "I've had so many men go through here… It could well be Victor's. Do you want more reasons to hang him over the mantle?"

Mark studied the framed photographs that decorated her bedroom walls. These appeared to depict Emilia's family and friends, but Victor did not appear among them.

"Well, no," he answered. "I was just wondering."

"Just don't fill gaps in knowledge with jealousy," she suggested. "What's taking you so long in there anyway?"

"I'm just looking at your photos." Mark focused on a series of them in which she was among a group in a folkloric dress. In the center was an older woman. "What do you mean, *filling the gaps with jealousy*?"

"Only that," she said, and after a pause added, "Victor is a sweet man and a good friend. His problem is in his intentions."

He gathered his clothes while searching for the gist of her aphorism. "I don't understand," he concluded.

The firewood crackled in the hearth, and it was the only sound he heard on returning to the living room. With a metal poker at hand, Emilia sat on the floor and incited the flames. *Beauty creates its own desire*, he remembered her suggesting, and the image of her by the fireplace was just that for him.

"Let me put it this way," she continued the discussion in a softer voice. "Love with Victor is love without grace."

His quest to find more details about Victor was evolving into a giant mental puzzle. At one time Mark would have thought *love without grace* was equivalent to tolerating a child with spilled egg yolk on their lapel. He clutched the crumpled clothes against his chest and silently mouthed her words, *love without grace*, but inflected it with the tone of a question.

"I've missed you," she said and turned to him. "I was afraid you had run off into the forest."

The glimmer from the flames in the hearth cast a shadow upon her silhouette that appeared to waver. Mark sat at the far end of the sofa as if mesmerized.

"I'm sorry. I was nosing through your photographs."

"Actually, they're like a journal of my life... as much as tangible memories of family and friends that always keep me company."

Mark envied her contented nostalgia. Of his own photographs, he kept them stored in a neglected closet, all haphazardly stowed in empty shoeboxes: often, these provoked recollections of failed dreams and the wreckage from time.

"Lay your clothes out on the sofa." She had set his sneakers to dry, raised on their heels and leaning against the rock platform of the fireplace. "Come sit by the fire so I can bandage your knee."

He stood up to sit where she patted the Middle Eastern rug. Facing the mantle, he asked, "Why is Bullwinkle grinning at me?"

With the sash tightened around the robe, he ensured the front flaps were snugly overlapped. Where he sat, the fire felt warm on his legs, stretched out toward where she prepared.

"Does Hansel make you insecure?" She asked, her legs were flexed under her when she threw open the garment over his knees. "What's this?" she asked and removed the washcloth. "You're still bleeding!"

"It had stopped when I applied pressure with that washcloth." Blood oozed from the wound where she prodded. Mark grimaced in anticipation of the pain her fingers threatened to cause.

"I don't know about this." She rose to her knees and bent over his leg. "I think we should go see a doctor."

"I trust you more than I would a doctor," he replied.

"Even if I'm just a pretend-nurse?"

"Being vulnerable is having to rely on trust?" Mark replied.

"Just what I didn't want to hear." Emilia let a solution drip into the wound that fizzled to a pink foam; she then dried its trickle with a swift swipe of gauze.

Mark remained still and, with the trust of a child, watched as her hair swayed with her movements over his wound. Neither the painful sting of the cleansing solution, nor her prodding, could distract him from recalling Emilia mention being at the side of her grandmother while assisting a neighbor to give birth.

Water boiled inside a black kettle, over the fire of a wood stove. Against a log wall, she sat in a far corner of the partly-lit room. Quietly, her feet dangled above the earthen floor as her fingers gripped the raw wood of the seat. Her pale skirt was unfurled to below her knees, and a thin leather ribbon bound her black hair from her face. Her hazel eyes were frightened and averted from the subdued cries of a woman giving birth. In the middle of the room, her grandmother knelt on a woven rug and, with outstretched arms, coaxed an infant from her mother's womb.

He recalled her warning, *don't fill gaps in knowledge with jealousy*; but at that moment, all he wished for was a laptop in which to type in the imagined details.

"There." Emilia capped the bottles of solution she had used to clean the wound. "Now don't be suing me if it gets infected."

"Is that your grandmother in the photo?" he asked.

"Which photo?"

"The old lady with the group in the folkloric dress."

"The old lady?" She increased the pressure she applied in dab-drying the wound, an obvious objection to his description.

"Ouch!" he responded. "So much for trust and vulnerability!"

"I just can't see her as 'the old lady,'" she smiled. "More as the wise woman... But yes, that's my grandmother."

"Was that taken in Georgia?"

"No. It was actually taken at the reservation in

Oklahoma."

"Aren't you from Georgia?"

"What's with all the personal questions?" Emilia sat back on the heels of her feet and laid out the bandage.

"Just wanted to fill in the gaps I don't know about you."

"What, you're feeling jealous?" She stopped with the preparation and returned his gaze.

"Yes, of your life before I met you."

"If it would be any solace, I am now what I was then."

"I suppose your religious studies makes it easier for you to speak in riddles." He leaned back onto his outstretched arms and watched her approximate the wound edges. "But tell me all about you, in the simple English of us infidels."

"Infidels?" she snickered. "A favorite catchword of missionaries attempting to convert the indigenous... And yes, my family is from Oklahoma. We only moved to Georgia after my mother's death."

"I'm sorry for your mother's death," he said and hesitated before adding, "as well as for choosing words having the wrong historical context... and who are the *we?*"

"My father, grandmother, and older brother." She wrapped the bandage around his knee. "To answer your next question: my father took us to Georgia because he believed my mother's spirit would await him in our ancestral lands."

"And that is in Georgia?"

"Yes, the southern Appalachians."

Emilia rose to her knees and whisked her hair to fall over one shoulder. Bent above his leg, she ran the bandage around his injured knee. On each turn of the bandage, her hand brushed the inside of his thigh. Sparkling with the reflection of flames dancing on logs, her eyes demurely glanced at him. She knotted the bandage but did not withdraw her hands.

Mark straightened to touch her. "You are beautiful," he heard himself say.

"And beauty makes you want more," she replied as if to repeat an invitation.

With the tenderness of an orchid in his hand, he drew her to his lips. Embraced, they rested upon the rug. He loosened the sash from around his waist and let the robe drop open. Hurriedly, she lifted her woolen sweater above her head and swept aside the disarray of hair that veiled her face.

In the flicker from the flames, their shadow appeared motionless, yet Mark felt as if he was racing to keep pace with the beat of his heart. He stroked her hair, seemingly splayed among the flowers of the rug. The sweat of their flesh shimmered as they eagerly indulged their impassioned yearning.

Mindlessly, he was jolted by a recurrent doubt of ever meriting pleasure. Subconsciously, he answered a rhetorical question: *it was from jealousy he coveted Emilia; he could not engage in love.*

Emilia's sigh was a subdued cry,
to that of a mother in post-labor.
A frightened child sat alone,
in the dark of a bedroom.

What defenses has a child,
but prayer against a threat?
Dark angels with painful tidings.
makes her vulnerable
when beholding trust.

A shudder of fear rushed through his body. Like inside a tightened noose, Mark felt himself become flaccid. In a desperate motion, he thrust his pelvis against hers, but only felt trapped between her legs. He slipped away from her hand which searched to help and furtively stroked himself.

Coals still glowed in the fireplace, but their heat was not the cause of the sweat he wiped away. The room became silent, except for her shallow breaths. On a glimpse, he noticed her nipples remained erect. Mark returned between her legs and, with the stroke of his tongue, tasted her flesh. As her breaths became more rapid, she rhythmically tightened her hold on his head until her taut muscles loosened into a shallow outburst.

Naked in a loose embrace, they slept until he was startled awake. *Love without grace*, he recalled her rebuke of Victor. On opening his eyes, Bullwinkle's grin filled the scope of his vision. *He knows the answer to the riddle*, he silently said, *and it's why he grins at me*. Gingerly, he removed his arm from under her head, but Emilia was awakened.

"I think my clothes are dry," he answered the question he expected.

"You don't have to go," she said. "Your clothes will be drier in the morning."

"I better get going." He tucked his shirt into his pants. "I have a lot to get done in the morning."

"Will you be at Maidu's for breakfast?" She covered up with the bathrobe.

Opening the front door, Mark stopped. An overcast moon was all that shone on the snow. "I'll try to make it," he said but did not look back.

Chapter 10

Emilia had given him affection, and what he had offered in return was a tease. But hindsight, he thought, was nothing more than the regret of having left her at the door. On the turn of the road back into the forest, he watched her image disappear from his rearview mirror; and before he had reached the highway into town, he reasoned it was better for him to vanish as well.

If to forget does not forgive, time allows for neglect: in the morning, he prepared to return to San Jose. With the blinds pulled down and the drapes shut, darkness could not hide her note still on top of the pyramid of coins. He folded the paper in four and stowed it in his shirt pocket.

By late morning, the traffic had thinned, and he followed it passed Maidu's Café. He glanced at the lot where the runoff from the perimeter snow-streaked across the pavement; he only slowed for the second it took the door to be slung shut behind a patron he didn't know.

At the park outside of town, more tire-tracks trekked the snow sludge into the parking lot, exposing black asphalt—a harbinger of spring. On the road south, he ascended into the forest and passed the side road to Emilia's cabin. *She's better off without me*, he concluded.

HWY 50 heading east was far from being a direct route home, but there was no rush to return. Instead, he was tempted to visit the caretaker's cottage in the ghost town of Bodie.

At the California border on HWY 375, a lonely Nevada casino jutted out from a barren hill and overlooked Lake Topaz in the saltine bed of a high desert valley. Mark knew the lake more as a mirage than a tranquil stretch of water, but he enjoyed its isolation.

Inside the small casino, the wooden walls reeked from years of cigarette smoke and the splatter of beer. An attendant stood at the single open game table. Except for the clang of silver coins being dropped into a slot, he detected no other gamblers. He continued past the casino to the coffee shop.

"Good morning!" said a waitress, wiping down the glass counter. "Sit wherever you like, honey."

The dining area was bright, with large windows facing the lake and the surrounding desert. Only one couple dined in the room, sitting across from each other at a table by the window. Mark sat two tables from them.

The waitress from the counter carried a meal to the couple's table. "Let's see, you had asked for the omelet," she said, placing the dish in front of the man, "and the lady ordered the steak an' eggs."

"You got it," the man replied. After a sip from a glass of beer, he took a drag of a cigarette and, with fork in hand, began to eat the breakfast. On his thin arm, below the rolled-up cuff of his T-shirt, Mark noticed a tattoo of a bare-chested hula dancer.

"Thanks," the female companion told the waitress on receiving her plate. Except for the woman's long hair and leather vest, she appeared her companion's mirror image.

"You want lunch or breakfast?" the waitress asked Mark.

"Breakfast," he answered, but continued to gaze at the couple.

"Honey, your face looks as long as I am wide," she laughed and handed him the breakfast menu. Rotund and appearing to be in her sixties, she bore a smile that was often accompanied by a musical chortle. It was difficult not to forgive her facial skin—appearing fissured with wrinkles from years of smoking.

"I was just thinking of how far I still have to go."

"Coffee?"

"Yes, please—Mildred," he read her nametag.

She went off to the service station and passed the couple eating in silence. Smoke curled from their cigarettes.

What keeps them entertained? Mark wondered.

Mildred returned to pour more coffee. "Where you goin'?"

"San Jose," he answered.

"No wonder the long face! You're *lost!*"

"No... I know. Just wanted to take a roundabout."

"Honey, this ain't no roundabout!" she chuckled. "You're lost... What're you havin'?" She pulled out the order check from her apron.

"I'll take the scrambled eggs breakfast."

"Yup—scrambled," she chuckled and tucked the order-check into her pocket, then carried the coffee pot into the kitchen.

"I think we'll make Las Vegas by sunset," Mark heard the man say.

"Shit! Are we stoppin' somewhere before then?" she asked. "My ass ain't gonna last on the back o' that bike!"

"Wish I had that Harley. Them Jap asses ain't as wide as what we got."

"Shit, your ass is no wider than my baby finger!"

"It ain't my baby *finger* that makes you howl like a whore!" the man answered and flicked his tongue rapidly into the beer.

Mark laughed at their banter and wondered if love could be so simple, or even as crass.

"Here you are," Mildred announced. "Scrambled eggs for a scrambled mind."

"Hey, wait a minute!" He pretended annoyance but accepted the basic tenet of what she claimed as his own. "Give me some credit... I made it here to see *you!*"

"Like I said, scrambled mind!" She laughed on her return to the counter.

The couple left, but Mark's stretch from the table did not allow him a peek at them packing onto the bike.

After three coffee refills, he paid the waitress at the counter.

"If it ain't a woman that's got you frazzled, it ain't worth the bother," Mildred added with the change.

"Thanks."

The game tables were all covered, and the slot machines were silent. The apparent solitude unnerved him, but he was determined to continue on the *roundabout* journey.

◆ ◆ ◆

From the desert valley, the highway ascended into the Sierra Nevada, where granite walls closed in on each other to form a canyon. Staggered boulders, one on top of the other, formed ledges that gave the palisades the appearance of a giant jigsaw puzzle.

Glancing at the vegetation, Mark noticed the pine

appeared similar to the Jeffrey trees of the peninsular park at Lake Tahoe. One tree attracted his attention—solitary and rooted in a crevice, high on the granite wall.

Do we become what we are destined? he recalled Emilia's question.

As if to find an answer, he pulled into a turnoff in line with the tree and scaled the rocks to where the tree was perched. There, he wedged his fingers into the crevice to feel how deeply the roots were embedded. From its precarious position, he realized the reason for the tree's survival: destiny had offered it the platform, but its tenacity provided for the nutrients.

He withdrew his hand and stared at the dark soil encrusting his fingernails. *Why are men like boys?* Emilia had asked; but realizing it was more a premonition, he countered with why they differed—*tenacity*. He shut his eyes and watched Emilia disappear from his rear-view mirror.

◆ ◆ ◆

Driving into his subdivision, Central San Jose appeared as a distant cluster of lights. In his neighbor's driveway was parked a red pickup that Mark assumed was the cop's new toy: *Maybe a trophy for warding off germs from the neighborhood.*

The mailbox was filled mostly with junk, which he discarded into the empty garbage can at the curb. Only a card from his mother, an envelope from his publisher, and a reminder note from his doctor was worth carrying into the house. On opening the front door, he was shaken by the foul odor of his last meal leftovers—mustard chicken he'd forgotten to refrigerate.

With all the windows open and a fan at full blast in the kitchen, he stared at the family of cats fronting his mother's card. In a few Spanish words, she expressed her unconditional love. *Ay querida!* he toyed with a dramatic reply.

In the publisher's envelope was a payment for the previous month's article and royalties for his most recent book. Disconcerting was the scorecard the publisher included, noting a drop-off in book sales and a reminder of his delinquency to provide the next article. He made a mental note to visit Arren in the morning.

The reason for the doctor's appointment was a mystery, but it would actually be convenient for having his knee wound checked. He rolled up the pant-leg and remembered Emilia applying the bandage: *There was no way the wound would get infected.*

In the den, he recognized the clutter on his desktop as a tiered accounting of his activity, as this was where he spent the most time. There was room enough only to place his laptop.

As if noticing it for the first time, he stared at a single framed photograph hanging across from the desk. It was of him posing with his mother, brother, and sister, but he could not recall the occasion.

At a far corner of the room and under a heap of tax records, Mark found the shoebox in which he had stowed photographs of family and friends. He sifted through the contents and laid them out in what he figured was chronological order: one day, it would facilitate arranging them for a *journal of his life.*

◆◆◆

In the 1990s, fledgling technology firms started their occupation of newly-built shiny glass structures in the perimeter of central San Jose, and these surrounded *American Publishing*—situated in a two-story downtown brick building since it was founded in 1918.

Mark enjoyed his visits to the publishing firm and considered these time-warped adventures. Were it not for the city council's efforts to prevent further demolition of historic structures, downtown San Jose would have been another ghost town for him to write about.

The firm had achieved moderate success in the publication of educational books, as well as magazines on esoteric subjects. *Western Ways* had become Mark's primary revenue source by distributing his articles to the niche market interested in Western Ghost Towns.

"Mark, you're not lost after all!" Betty shouted from across the editor's reception area while watering the window plants. "I've called you many times and left messages… I was worried."

"I was up at the lake. Thanks for the worry, but sorry—I didn't get the messages."

Betty was the editor's secretary to whom he often reported his whereabouts.

"You're looking good in red," he added.

"Thanks." She spread the skirt of her red-dotted shirtdress as if for a reassuring second look. "Arren has been wanting to talk to you."

"Uh, oh… What haven't I done?"

"He didn't say what it's about, but I think it wasn't important… His voice would have given it away." She returned to behind her desk and fingered a scheduler. Looking up to Mark, she added, "Something about you seems different… Is everything okay?"

"Seems I haven't been looking my best lately." He sat down on the sofa. "Even the waitress at a desert café told me I looked *scrambled*."

"Let me know if there's anything I can do… I'll get

Arren." She reached for the phone but stopped when Arren walked in from the front.

"Mark, where have you been? Have you been talking to Betty?" Arren continued into his office, and Mark followed. "Isn't she wonderful?... I've been wanting to chat with you."

With a hand to Mark's shoulder, Arren led him to the chair facing the heavy mahogany desk at the center of the room. Twenty-two years previously, Mark had taken Arren's literature course at UCLA, and their relationship had not transcended beyond that of a student to his instructor—Mark was intimidated.

"What do you think of Betty?" Arren leaned forward, as if to disclose a secret, and added, "How would you like to go on a date with her?" He lifted a single bushy eyebrow and fell back to his chair. His stare was magical as if with the power to grant a wish.

Mark searched for a hyphen, better yet an exclamation point. He wanted to extend the pause before he answered. "What are you saying?"

Arren folded his hands on the edge of the desk and sat deeper in the chair. He would have to negotiate. "You know my wife, Susan, the matchmaker. She found out Betty was not dating, so they went out for lunch a few days ago. You know—*preliminary compatibility review*. Anyway, to cut the fat, it turns out Betty wants you."

The Ansel Adams photograph of the Half Dome behind Arren was hypnotic. It was a while before Mark moved his stare from it. "I'm old enough to be her father," he said in a quiet tone.

"Not really... just an older brother," he replied. "She's twenty-eight."

"She's a sweet woman," Mark added with his stare back to the dome.

"And quite a good looker." The gleam in Arren's eyes assured he would accept no challenges.

"Arren, what would Susan say if she knew about your lust?"

"After forty-one years and three sons, she knows I'm a window-shopper." He paused and more soberly added, "But look at you, Mark. You're middle age. What is it now, forty-two? You're successful, and you're a good man. But you don't enjoy life. You wear blinders all the time."

It was not the first time Arren had plotted to fix Mark with a date; but it was the first time there was an urgency in his tone.

"You're right," Mark replied.

"I don't mean to get down on you, but cut yourself some slack!" He stood up from the chair and walked past Mark, who followed to the door. "Heck, what's the use of being Jewish if I can't be a yenta?"

"Thanks for the concern."

They shook hands.

"Did you bring in the article for next month's issue?" Arren asked at the door, his tone that of a professor at the podium.

"Not yet, but soon."

Arren closed the door behind him.

Betty was seated on her chair but bent forward to below the desktop. She appeared to pick at something on the floor.

"Did you get it all?" Mark asked.

"I spilled my money." The purse rested upright on her lap. "I was just counting it out to go get some yogurt for lunch, the phone rang, and I dropped the purse, but

I think I got it all." She took a second look around the floor below the desk.

"Don't worry... I'll take it as my opportunity to take you out to lunch."

"You don't have to," she said. "I'm sure I have enough." She opened the palm of her hand and revealed four quarters.

◆◆◆

He thought of the mound of snow that had remained on the deck in Lake Tahoe, probably melted by now. The sun was sure to be as brilliant there as it was on their walk to the restaurant, one block from the publishing firm.

Betty had folded a sweater over her forearm but left her purse locked in her desk. "It's a beautiful day," she said. "How was it at the lake?"

"A storm dumped a lot of snow just before I arrived, but it was starting to melt by the time I left." He held the door open.

"It must be beautiful," she responded on entering.

"Let's eat outside." He answered the hostess at the entrance. "Do you mind?" he asked Betty.

"Not at all," she responded and followed them to the table. Against the gentle breeze, Betty grabbed her hair into a bun and secured it with a clip. "It really is a lovely day."

"Is that a butterfly?" he asked, gazing at her hair clip.

"Yes," she answered, and then added, "I'm surprised you didn't inform us you were heading up to the lake... I imagined you wandering alone in some ghost town."

"Or kidnapped by a band of *Indians...?*" He felt as if dropped into a cliff. "Oops, wrong phrase... Sorry." He hesitated before continuing. "I'm sorry; I should have informed you… It was just on the spur of the moment."

"You know how Arren worries about you. Just give him a heads-up next time… By the way, what was it he wanted?"

Mark hesitated. "Oh… he was just concerned about my being late with the next article."

It took him as much effort to eat the dry French Dip sandwich as to carry a conversation. He was relieved when Betty noticed it was time to return.

"Sorry I was not much of a conversationalist." He held open the door into the brick building. "I am starting to get worried about being so late on my next article for Arren."

"I understand, but I did enjoy our time together. Maybe we can have lunch again… when you're finished with the article."

He was glad for the deadline as an excuse to sequester himself for the following few days. "We should definitely do it again," he said and let the door close behind her.

Chapter 11

Inspiration is rarely granted in a vacuum, as by a muse; but rather, it is worked for. The labor to achieve it often becomes a ritual, as it had for Mark.

The topics to write about frequently developed from what he had read or memorialized. On the recliner by his reference library, shelved in a full-wall bookcase in the living room, he would search for the historical facts to enrich his imagination; and so he began the research to develop Sadie's background.

Soon frustrated in finding minimal information on the Cherokee Nation, he realized the focus of his books was primarily on western ways. He did find a historical accounting of indigenous Sierra Nevada tribes. Shuffling through the pages, he came upon an essay on the Maidu tribe in the central Sierra Nevada. He sat deep into a leather sofa and read as if for a mystical brew.

These were an aboriginal people of northeastern California, whose sustenance reminded him of the solitary pine tree rooted on the granite perch: their survival was in the balance of destiny and tenacity. *What was it like*, he wondered, *to be truly vulnerable?*

The eventual extinction of the tribe was not described, but Mark filled the gap with what he knew well. Miners and loggers from around the world encroached upon their lands and, with superior technology, eventually displaced the Maidu.

Mark sat at his laptop. The clutter on his desk remained unaffected. As if reaching across the gap of time, he stretched his hands to type on the keyboard. It was his first tale of an aboriginal people in the Old West.

◆◆◆

Sadie

Against a log wall, Sadie sat on a chair. The skirt of her dress was unfurled to below the knees. Her bare feet dangled over the earthen floor, and her fingers gripped the raw wood of the seat. Strands of her black hair were bound back from the face with a thin leather ribbon. She remained quiet; her eyes turned away from the subdued sounds of a woman giving birth.

The room was dim, partly lit by the fire in the corner stove. In a lead kettle, water boiled. On a tulle mat in the middle of the floor, Sadie's grandmother knelt between the woman's legs and coaxed, with outstretched hands, the infant from the mother's womb.

Silence was followed by the shrill cry of the newborn child. Sadie turned to see her grandmother place the infant on the mother's naked abdomen. "It's a boy," she joyously proclaimed.

At her mother's hearty laugh, Sadie relaxed her grip of the seat and looked curiously at her brother. His black hair glistened with moisture. Patches of red coalesced with a thin mush that coated his skin.

The grandmother tied the fleshy cord that extended from her brother's belly and hid between her mother's legs. A gush of blood splattered when she cut the cord.

Her brother, wrapped in a rabbit skin blanket, was pacified as he suckled on his mother's breasts.

"Pour some water into that basin," the grandmother directed Sadie.

Quick to jump out of her chair, Sadie did as she was told. With both arms, she lifted the kettle off the stove and set it on the floor. She leaned over it with caution and poured the boiling water into the basin.

"Use the hide to wipe your brother clean," the grandmother added as she tugged at the cord, still hidden between the mother's legs. Sadie noted the concern in her grandmother's stare.

At the end of a stick, the rabbit's hide was dipped into the water. When the hide cooled, Sadie wiped off the thick film that coated her brother's skin. The olive color of her flesh contrasted with her brother's light pink.

"Push!" her grandmother loudly commanded.

Her mother grunted in response. Sadie looked up and noticed pain in her mother's face, and yet the infant continued to suckle at the breast.

"Get him on the bed!" the grandmother shouted.

Blood had pooled at her grandmother's knees, and more continued to stream from between her mother's legs. Sadie remembered her fear when she first smelled that scent, the day her father had skinned a brown bear. She rushed to her brother and carried him to the bed.

The grandmother let the cord drop to wash her arms with the rabbit's hide. She buried her hand in the mother's womb and tugged on the cord with her free hand—the mother's muted cry blended with the grandmother's pleas to push. The child wailed from the head of the bed.

Sadie did not recognize the silence that followed a burgundy mass being pulled from the womb, but the stream of blood ceased to flow. Beads of sweat on her mother's face shimmered in the glow of the fire. Sadie sat still on the edge of the bed and waited for her grandmother's command.

"Evelyn?" the grandmother asked softly.

The stillness that followed shook Sadie's body. Her mother was pale, as she had never been before. The tulle mat at her grandmother's knees was lost in a solid redness that frightened her. The smell of blood was nauseating.

"Bring me your brother." Her mother's words echoed loudly in Sadie's ears.

The grandmother assisted Evelyn to sit, and Sadie handed her the infant to feed.

"Sadie, come help me." She held the placenta for her grandmother to fold with the mat, then moistened the hide to wash her mother's body. Wrapped in a blanket, her mother was supported to the bed, and the child was allowed to sleep on his mother's breast.

The folded mat was cautiously inserted into the basket her grandmother had woven over the last month of the pregnancy. Decorated with black and yellow bird feathers, it would later be buried. Sadie slept at her mother's feet.

◆ ◆ ◆

The grandmother stoked the flames in the stove as steam billowed from the covered kettle. Sadie awakened to the late winter cold frosting her face.

"Would you like tea?" asked her grandmother.

"Has mother taken any?" She took in a whiff of the manzanita scent.

"No, she's tired from the birth of your brother. She'll take some soon."

Her mother lay still in bed, but Sadie watched the slow rise of the blanket over her chest. Visible above the hem was a tuft of her brother's black hair. She listened to him whimper as he was fed.

Sadie scooted out of bed and spread her blanket over her mother's legs, then covered her seven-year-old frame with the deerskin coat her father had made. The door out from the hut was just her height.

The winter had not been harsh, but the ground was still spotted with a thin layer of snow. She preferred to walk barefoot and feel the trail she could not see in the dim morning light.

It was a new world, but on her walk, she imagined it like when her father had been with them. Then, they had lived at the edge of the forest, where her mother tilled the flat land about their home. Her father had fished and hunted in the woods.

At the end of spring, her father had staggered out of the forest and fell into the vegetables her mother tended. Blood stained the skin of his chest.

Four light-skinned men followed from the trees, and her mother screamed for her to run into the forest. Hidden in her father's sweat-house, Sadie waited.

When the sun rested below the crown of trees, her mother appeared with her face scratched and the dress torn from her breast.

Her grandmother soon followed. Behind her, she pulled the travois used to carry wood from the forest. On it was her father, with his chest motionless and covered red with blood.

In the river that ran past the sweathouse, the three women washed her father's body, as her grandmother chanted a song Sadie had heard at the death of other villagers. Tears blurred her vision as they marched away from their home: remembering her father's body left in a shallow grave.

◆◆◆

The rise on the trail from the hut was Sadie's preferred spot to watch the sunrise. When daylight outlined the crest of the mountains to the east, the last star to the west she knew to be her father's. At night, his shone among all her ancestors.

On the rise, she squatted behind a gooseberry shrub and listened to her urine stream into the canyon, then fall onto the rocky shore of the river below. That morning, Sadie prayed that her father would protect her mother.

On her return, Sadie whispered the song her grandmother had chanted at the burial of her father: it called on a white man's spirit to guide his soul.

From the trail, the steeple of the Presbyterian Church loomed high above their hut. Before her father's death, the family had taken up Christian ways; it was how they had obtained their city names. After his death, when their food stores had been exhausted, and the winter cold kept them from farming, the minister and his family had given them shelter.

On her return, confident every spirit had been alerted to her prayers, Sadie thought to get more fuel for the stove. Her mother and brother needed to be kept warm.

As her father had taught her, she took for fuel only those branches littering the forest. The townspeople, though, simply cut down the trees and kept larger stocks of wood. Sadie decided to carry an armful from the stack of logs the minister had placed against their hut.

Voices from the road into town stopped her at the door. It was of men she knew were waiting for a horse-drawn carriage to take them to the mines, deep inside the canyon. Her mother called them *white-skins*, but Sadie had noticed some with flesh the shade of hers, others as dark as cedar trees.

Initially frightened with so much that was new, she eventually became intrigued. There were those like her, with a slant to the eyes, but whom she didn't understand. Some had hair as yellow as the sun, and others with eyes of sky blue. At the church school, she learned the language of the townspeople, and everyone became a friend. Writing, though, fascinated her most: that she could carry a message and not ever have to speak a word.

On entering, it appeared her mother still slept but had not moved since Sadie had left. She dropped the lumber by the stove and ran to the foot of the bed.

"Let her rest," the grandmother warned. On her lap was the basket, into which she wove more colorful bird feathers. "Now go get ready, and let Reverend Calhoun know your mother gave birth to a boy, but won't be working today."

◆◆◆

The grandmother held the basket to her chest and carried it outside. Following the trail Sadie had taken, she rejoiced for her prayers being answered in granting a son.

Not long after the arrival of the white man to their ancestral lands, fewer village children were born. Many of the villagers blamed the cloudy river waters flowing from the white man's mines.

On his first visit to their village, Reverend Calhoun told the villagers a Christian tale of a virgin mother and a patient father. Even after four barren spring times since being united to her husband, and not long after the reverend's sermon, she became pregnant and bore a son. She named him Joseph, *the patient one*, and took the name of Margaret in gratitude.

Eventually, the Christian villagers followed the reverend into town to work the mines, and the non-believers migrated to where the water ran clear. After the death of her husband, Margaret remained in the land of her ancestors to venerate his spirit. Joseph married Evelyn, and Sadie was their only child.

◆◆◆

Margaret stopped at a rise in the trail and walked to

the edge of the canyon. She stared across it to where the forest remained as her ancestors knew it, and where their spirits still dwelled. From the ground where she stood, she picked a firm cedar twig and sharpened it to dig a small burial site into the hard earth.

Life continued into death, she thought, but to bury her son had challenged her new-found Christian faith. To prepare his spirit's journey, she had cried over his body with the howl of a wolf. Of the few Christian prayers she had learned, she chanted the one recited in church and was accompanied by wind chimes.

After her husband's death, Evelyn missed her monthly bleed and knew it could only be the white man's seed inside her. It was on the promise her husband's death would be avenged on the birth of a son that Margaret dissuaded her from suicide.

Inside the nativity basket, Margaret carried the afterbirth. She solemnly placed it into the earthen cavity she had dug and lightly covered it with gravel. The scent, she silently prayed, would entice a roaming wolf to carry it among her ancestors and, from there, her son's revenge would be fulfilled.

Sadie sat at the edge of the bed but did not turn to look at her grandmother's return. She held a cup of tea to her mother's lips and smiled when she took a sip.

"You must go on to Mrs. Calhoun," Margaret said from the door. "I'll help your mother drink the tea."

Sadie went off to the Calhoun home as directed, and there she anticipated writing an announcement of her brother's birth. In hopes of sharing her thoughts, she planned to keep the note with her all day; but as soon as Mrs. Calhoun answered her knock on the door, Sadie was directed to her cleaning chores.

Rushing through her duties only left idle time before school would begin. Once in class, she regretted having learned to tell time, as all she could do was slowly count the minutes until the ring of the bell would release her for home.

"Sadie!" shouted Mrs. Calhoun from the podium after the bell rang. Sadie stopped in mid-stride and waited for a scolding. "Let me come with you… I want to visit your mother."

◆ ◆ ◆

Mrs. Calhoun led Sadie by the pull of her hand, past the door and into the hut. Instantly, they loosened their grip on noticing the grandmother at the edge of the bed, cradling the infant in one arm and wiping beads of sweat on the mother's forehead.

"Oh, my!" Mrs. Calhoun proclaimed as Sadie attempted to re-establish a hold of her hand. "Oh, poor darling!" Mrs. Calhoun said on touching the mother's forehead. "She's with a bad fever. I must get the doctor."

A breeze followed her out that smelled of roses. Things would be better, Sadie thought on remembering that roses grow only in spring. Quietly, she sat on the chair at the head of the bed and waited for Mrs. Calhoun to return.

He appeared much younger than the Calhouns standing next to him, but the doctor took charge on entering the hut. Her grandmother stepped back from the bed to let him pass.

"She's burning up!" The doctor withdrew his hand from her face and quickly lifted the blanket from above her mother's lower body. He parted her legs and whispered as if only for himself to hear, "She's not bleeding… it's probably not a retained placenta."

Sadie looked up to her mother on hearing her moan with the doctor's touch of her abdomen; she winced on her mother's yelp of pain when he inserted his long white fingers into her womb.

"It's post-partum sepsis," he proclaimed.

"What can we do to help her?" the Calhouns asked.

"Pray… There's not much else I can offer." He opened the black purse he had carried in. "Her body will have to fight the infection… Give her this for the fever," he handed the grandmother two labeled vials containing a white powder. "And this for pain."

"She doesn't understand English," Mrs. Calhoun said when the grandmother hesitated. "I'll let Sadie instruct her on the directions."

"Good. Call me when the fever breaks." The doctor clipped the purse shut and walked out of the hut.

Sadie understood every word they had spoken, but not what they meant. She listened to Mr. Calhoun lead a short prayer she had heard on sad occasions.

"Amen!" Sadie held back from shouting the response.

"Sadie, tell your grandmother we must take the child with us. Your mother won't be able to feed him," Mrs. Calhoun said in reaching for her brother. "Tom Lopez will lend us his nursing goat."

From the tone in their voices, Margaret understood the gloom revealed on their faces. With trust in the spirits of her ancestors and the charity of the Calhouns, she surrendered the last male of her people.

◆◆◆

Under a solitary cedar tree, Sadie remained motionless in her stiff new shoes but wished to be barefoot and feel the pebbles beneath her feet. In the sunlight, a warm breeze drifted from the forest across the canyon.

That morning, she had helped wash her mother's skin and draped her with a dress—fashioned from deerskin her father had hunted the previous spring. A beaded necklace, in the colors of butterflies, adorned her mother.

Wrapped in a white cotton blanket, her brother suckled noisily from a bottle. Cradled in her arms, his grandmother watched him, and Mrs. Calhoun stood behind them.

The reverend read from the scriptures—words to guide her mother's soul. Two dark-skinned men lowered the pine box in which her mother rested, deep into the ground. Gravel was shoveled over it, and Sadie prayed her mother's spirit could still escape from the enclosure.

Sadie held back howling like a wolf: it was a different world in which she would need to guide her brother. With the palm of her hand, she wiped away her tears.

◆◆◆

Mark sat back from the laptop, satisfied Sadie's prospect for success was strengthened by *trust*.

On Monday, he would take the article to Arren.

Chapter 12

He pushed away from the keyboard and wondered if Emilia would judge his interpretation of Sadie's life a *faux pas*: politically sensitive, but in the wrong social context. He'd managed to do that often enough since meeting Emilia. But after editing the story a number of times, he was proud to claim it complete.

Three stripes of the afternoon sunlight were formed on the wooden floor in his den. He stared up from them to the window as if to gaze through the bars of a prison. Writing had always forced him into isolated concentration, but thinking of Emilia created a longing to be with company.

Cut yourself some slack, he recalled Arren advise him.

Mark approached the window and drew open the blinds. "Hi, Kathy," he said into the phone. "Is Spencer in?"

"Hi... Who's this?" Kathy asked.

"It's Mark Balcon."

"Oh, sure," she replied hesitantly. "Haven't seen you in a while. He's upstairs. Let me get him."

After a few minutes, Spencer came on the line, "Hey, bud. What's up?"

"Hi, Spencer. How are the war games?"

"Okay, I guess. I was actually on the 'net, trying to dominate the world."

"Just wanted to see if you were in for a commando mission tonight?" Mark asked.

"Kathy and the kids are back, and she's not going to let me go," Spencer answered. "By the way, how did it go with that babe?"

'Babe' and 'bud' were Spencer's well-worn colloquialism that annoyed Mark. "What babe?"

"At the Seoul Lounge... I didn't think you were going to follow her upstairs... but it made me proud you did," Spencer added.

The tryst seemed a distant memory, but Mark recalled his police-neighbor considered it a threat to the neighborhood. "That's right... I don't remember you coming to my rescue," Mark said to Spencer.

"Man, I wasn't going to wait while you got your jollies off," Spencer replied. "I'm a married man—would've been too much temptation."

How sad, Mark held back from interjecting his assessment. After a period of numbing conversation, he ended, "Call me."

The sound of children at play distracted Mark to the window at the front of the house. In the cul-de-sac in which he lived, it would only be coming from the next-door neighbor's home.

Two small girls about the age of five chased each other on the neighbor's front lawn. The red-haired girl he assumed was the cop's daughter. *Fredrickson* was what he remembered the second officer call his neighbor at the Seoul Lounge.

"Don't go out on the street," Fredrickson said to the girls who had run to the curb. His voice lacked the peal with which he had commanded Mark against the wall.

Fredrickson stood up from behind the new pickup and walked around to Mark's full view. With the slow spray from the water hose at hand, he squatted to scrub the rear wheel. He wore only shorts and a T-shirt.

"Honey, I got you a beer." An attractive woman, in jeans and a T-shirt, walked out of the open garage carrying two beer cans. The cop stood up and reached for the can she handed him, and as he did, a chance spray of water from the hose soaked her chest. "Oh, Christ!" she shouted.

"Oh, yeah!" Fredrickson blurted out on noticing the accentuated outline of her breasts on the moistened T-shirt. "I know what I'd rather have."

Seductively, she approached him and brushed her breasts gingerly against his chest. When he attempted an embrace, she grabbed his hand that held the dripping nozzle and forced it down inside the front of his shorts. "Chill it, Eric… I got your newborn son to feed."

Children at play was the comforting sound that persisted when he sat back in the living room recliner. Lulled into the memory of a Sunday drive and games with his dad in the jungle gym, he rested.

On a glance at the phone, Mark tried to recall the last call he had received. *Wasn't it from Mamacita?* he asked to mock the question, then picked up the phone and dialed.

"Is Betty in?"

"Hi, Mark," she answered. "Who else would be answering this phone?"

"I don't know. I was just surprised to find you at home instead of being outside on such a beautiful day."

"It sure has been beautiful, but I had a few chores to take care of," she replied. "I'm glad you called but was it to procrastinate, or just taking a break?"

"Matter of fact, neither. I actually finished the article in record time… just so I could call you sooner."

"I should be flattered, but somehow I don't believe I was the mainspring for your call."

"Don't tell me you don't believe me?"

"Actually, I do believe you," she said and sounded less mischievous when she added, "because you seem more compassionate since returning from your recent trip to the lake."

"Well, I'm not sure if I should take it as being complimentary." He suspected hers was a reference to the frazzled state the coffee shop waitress had observed. "One thing I now intend never to do again is ignore a beautiful woman… Can I invite you to dinner?"

"I had a talk with Arren on Friday, and he told me what he had said to you." After a long pause, she gleefully added, "but I couldn't think of an argument against what he plotted, even if it will require some arm-twisting."

Arren had commented that Mark's age difference with Betty was no greater than that of an older brother. Though, looking himself over in the mirror, he realized the four-day beard made him appear more paternal. After a shave, a rugby shirt, and casual pants, he hoped to have trimmed off a few years.

The bebop jazz on the radio paced his drive to the restaurant Betty had selected. He arrived at about sunset and just as Betty stepped out of her car.

"I see your mother chose your wardrobe," she greeted him.

"Why?" He checked that his zipper was closed.

"You have that preppy look mothers like their sons to wear. I was kind of expecting the rough look of a cloistered monk."

"Just wanted to impress you." He looked her up and down. "You know, Arren is right," he said and held her arm at the elbow, "only a fool would disregard a beautiful woman like yourself."

Betty had her auburn hair twisted into two loose temple braids she had joined in the back with a butterfly pin. She wore an embroidered red silk blouse over a lilac skirt. Her athletic leg extended through the side slit of her dress.

"You said I looked good in red." She pirouetted on their walk into the restaurant. "So here you have it!"

Her abrupt turn surprised him, and he reached as if to catch her. "Dancing would be fun?" he suggested with his arm around her waist.

"Maybe after dinner," Betty said and followed the hostess into the restaurant.

Their table was alongside a front window, but a large Boston fern screened their view of the parking lot. A floodlight on the plant's underside directed his focus to its finger-like projections. "That's one of my favorite plants," Mark said.

"Sexually self-sufficient," she commented.

"Oh my!" Mark replied and quickly wiped his forehead to feel the warmth of a blush. Was it a botanical equivalent of *Love without grace?* "I didn't mean it because of that reason."

"I'm sorry," she laughed. "It just popped into my mind when I noticed the spores."

With the menu at hand, he stared as if at a blank paper. "If only it could be that easy," he quietly mentioned.

Betty remained silent while studying the menu, but was quick to reply when the waitress returned for their order. "I'll take the salmon," she requested.

"It's marinated in garlic and wine," Mark read of the salmon she ordered. "It does sound like a pretty good choice... I'll take it as well," he said to the waitress.

"That's twice we've ordered the same meal." Betty returned the menu to the waitress and clasped her hands over the table. "Let's make this more interesting— what's your article about?" she asked.

"Vulnerability and trust," he answered.

She dropped onto the backrest of the chair. "Is that like Roy Rogers and Trigger?" she asked with a chuckle. "Don't you always focus your articles on miners and cowboys?"

"Actually, come to think of it, being vulnerable is a common theme for my characters. And those that succeed in their struggles do so mostly because of a reliance on trust."

"When did this insight come to you?" Betty appeared to appease a suspicion when she added, "In Lake Tahoe?"

"I suppose so." Mark fiddled with the silverware and worked to mimic Bullwinkle's grin. "Do you know what *Love without grace* is?" he asked but kept his focus on the silverware.

"Love without grace?" she repeated slowly as if to search for a meaning between the letters. After a sip of water, she concluded, "I may have heard it in a song, but I'm not sure. Does it have to do with being vulnerable and trusting?"

"It could well be," he answered. "As far as I know, it's a riddle, or maybe a cryptic poetic prose."

"I suppose if you knew the poet, it would be easier to figure it out," she said.

Mark appreciated the change of subject when the waitress delivered the meal.

"Would you like anything else?" asked the waitress.

"I think white wine would go well with the salmon," Betty suggested.

"How about a Riesling?" Mark asked the waitress, who jotted it on the order pad as a request and marched off.

It was not long before she returned with the wine to fill their glasses. Mark raised his for a toast. "To a poet's reproach, offered as a riddle!"

"No worries unless it's a rebuke!" She raised her glass to his and sipped the wine.

"Sounds like wise advice," he replied.

"Just something to think about." Betty held back on a second sip and returned the glass to the table. "I've told you how you recently appear different."

"Yes... *more compassionate* is what you said," he answered as he prodded with a fork the recently delivered salad.

"Maybe more... delightfully vulnerable."

"What?" he responded with a chuckle. "You mean like a preppy kid wearing the clothes his mother laid out for him?"

"Maybe more like the preppy kid wanting his mother's approval." It was Betty's turn to blush.

Their entrées were set in front of them. Mark stared at the sautéed salmon dripping garlic butter and recalled watching them swim upstream in Seattle, along a channel built to the side of a dam. Instinct, he thought, had provided their passion to swim against the powerful flow of water. Their tenacity, he assessed, was genetically determined... whereas, his would need to be acquired.

"I had a good time, thank you," Betty said getting into her car. With the door pulled shut, she advised Mark through the open window, "You need to go back to the poet and ask what *'love without grace'* means."

Alvarado

Chapter 13

Gentrification appeared to be in slow progress for the section of downtown where the medical office was located. Metal bars protected the front windows of the small building and, from where Mark glanced, it was the primary form of security for the rest of the neighborhood. He recognized it as the urban decay that, if left unchecked, would result in a ghost town similar to those he wrote about.

Surprised at the apparent decline since his last visit, Mark glared at the graffiti-painted boards that sealed off the emptiness of adjoining structures. He was tentative on entering the medical building and was rattled when an electric chime announced his entry.

It was about five years since his last visit to Dr. Chen, and he could not recall why he had made the appointment shortly before setting out to Lake Tahoe. It, though, turned out to be opportune as the wound on his knee was healing slowly.

The room he entered took him into a different world from a different era than from where he had come: bulky American Colonial furniture of cherrywood cluttered the waiting area. Except for a Chinese porcelain lamp and Persian rug, everything appeared to be where he recalled it last being.

Dr. Chen's California family roots were as deep as

the goldmines' need for labor. Mark supposed the Oriental touches celebrated an ancestral bond—just as he imagined was the reason for Emilia's travels to religious studies in Berkeley. He hoped Sadie's tale honored those bonds, and looked forward to submitting the article to Arren later that afternoon.

A small service window with glazed glass slid open on the wall opposite where he entered. Mark was startled.

"Are you Mark Balcon?" asked a young woman.

"Yes," he replied.

"We need your file updated," the voice from the window commanded.

An arm then displaced her face and stretched out to hand him a clipboard.

At the leather chair, a dim light from the adjacent porcelain lamp was sprayed upon the sheet he held listing an array of personal questions. On reviewing options given for associated symptoms, *recurrent chills* reminded him of what had prompted him to make the appointment: an episode had recently caused him to hide behind cardboard boxes at the supermarket while spurning assistance from an attendant.

"Excuse me?" He rapped the pencil on the glass and watched a profile of a woman swell behind the glaze. The window slid open. "I'm finished," he said.

"Thank you." The arm projected towards him and, as swiftly, withdrew the clipboard. The young face reappeared. "Please have a seat. Mrs. Wright will be with you shortly."

From where he sat, the bulky chairs of the waiting room appeared somber with no one sitting on them. The chairs conjured up gothic images and tales from Edgar Allan Poe. While in a silent recital of *The Raven*, Mark was bolted to his feet by a bellow that came from behind him.

"Good morning, I'm Mrs. Wright." A corpulent woman with a contralto voice greeted him. She held the rear door open with her broad buttocks. White teeth filled her smile. "I'm your nurse. Follow me."

The antiseptic white of her uniform contrasted sharply with the ebony of her skin. A brilliant gold cross hung from her neck, suspended in the deep cleavage of her voluminous breasts. Framed by sterile white walls, she led him down a short corridor to a balance scale.

"Take your shoes off," she directed, then added, "Stand against the bar."

She balanced the weights, then extended the bar to the crown of his head. She called out the measures as if at an auction, "One hundred and eighty pounds, six feet."

He drew in his girth for her to wrap a tape around his waist. "Thirty-two inches," she continued, "… with an inch sucked in!"

He followed barefoot into a small room and waited at an exam bed set against a windowless wall. "Undress to your underwear and put this on." She handed him a paper gown and closed the door on her exit.

He clipped the gown at the front and bent forward to the floor where he laid the clothes in a pile.

"Honey, that butt is a fine view," Mrs. Wright observed from the door, "but you'll have to show more to get my review."

After taking his blood pressure and placing a thermometer under his tongue, she noted, "You're awful quiet… Scared of doctors?"

"It's hard to talk from inside this paper bag—and now you have a rod in my mouth." The thermometer bobbed with his response.

"Son, be glad it ain't up your butt!" she laughed. "Now, lay back and let me take an EKG."

The examination table was as hard and cold as a butcher's slab. After the nurse's prodding and number calling, he could sympathize with the disgrace a cow went through.

Mrs. Wright pulled back the front of the gown. "Honey, I be blessed! You ain't got hairs on your chest."

"And what are those?" He pointed to a few strands of hair.

"Those, my boy, are *wannabes!*" She attached the EKG cables to aluminum strips systematically placed on his chest. "Now stay still so I can record the rhythm of your heart… You Spanish boys got rhythm, don't you?" Her breasts jiggled with her laughter.

Mark remained motionless as directed. "Mrs. Wright," he sighed, "I think you're making fun of me."

"There, got it. You can move now." She stared at the electrical squiggles on the recording paper. "It looks like prime meat to me… Don't get me wrong, baby. I'm just an old dog that likes a good tease. Now stick your arm out."

"What's that for?" He stared at the syringe she handled.

"It's suppertime!" Without hesitation, she tightened a tourniquet around his upper arm and quickly pricked the blue cord that filled under the skin at his elbow. When the syringe was filled with blood, she held it up for inspection, "Kind of thin, ain't it?"

"All of this torture, just to have my wound checked?" he asked.

"Paper says you're here for a mid-life physical," she said, pointing to a clipboard on the writing table. "That's a complete work-up. You ain't goin' to go chicken, are you?"

Mid-life was a crisis; whereas, middle age he defined as an epoch. Either term, he thought, referred to a life half-lived. The absoluteness of his place in time did tempt him to *go chicken*.

"Dr. Revels will be in shortly," Mrs. Wright said as she exited.

"Who's Dr. Revels?" he asked as the door was shut, but kept a focus on his reflection in the mirror that hung over the sink, across from the examining bed. *Age is an incessant artist,* he thought and outlined the creases on his forehead, *each wrinkle an indelible stroke of its brush.*

"Hello, I'm Dr. Danielle Revels," said an attractive woman entering the examination room. "Looks like Kathleen has been at her taunting again…"

"Hello, Dr. Revels."

"Please call me Danielle."

"Hello, Dr. Danielle." He turned back to the examination table. "Was just brushing something from my eye."

"By chance, was it age?" she asked from the writing table, where Mrs. Wright had left the clipboard and EKG tracing.

The doctor's white coat was open at the front. A fuchsia tunic dress was noticeable between the flaps. She was thin, but her smock filled the outline of her figure. Long brunette hair was draped over her left shoulder in a ponytail. She seemed too young to be a doctor.

"Wh-where is Dr. Chen?" he stammered.

"I bought into his practice two years ago, and he recently retired." Danielle reviewed the data on the clipboard. "I hope you don't mind. I'm fully boarded in internal medicine."

"No, no. It's fine. I've just never had a woman doctor."

"Well, good; then please have a seat on the examination bed," she said without looking away from the questionnaire. "So, you're a writer?"

"Yes." He wished he hadn't checked 'yes' on the option *if ever failed at an erection*.

"What do you write?"

"Articles for a specialty magazine... and short stories."

"You've never been married?" She looked up from the clipboard. "Is it an issue of insecurities? Or being gay?"

"Not much tact in your questions," he retorted. "I hope you realize there are many more options... Would you accept that it's more convenient for me in this stage of my life?"

Emilia, when at the lake, had asked him whether he thought *we make our own destiny* or *become what we are destined*. At that moment, he supposed convenience had allowed him to waver. But before the doctor's offered options, he had not considered his loneliness to have been a choice, until he realized the comfort it provided him.

"I'm sorry being upfront, but sometimes tact clouds the issue, and a person's sexuality is of medical significance." She stood up and prepared to examine him. "Your only medical concern today is the wound on your knee?"

"Yes... I actually had forgotten I'd made this appointment."

The doctor began her examination with Mark seated at the edge of the bed. The gentle probing of her fingers in his scalp soothed him. "It's been a while since your last physical, and by our protocol, you need a mid-life evaluation. We consider that to include a physical and emotional assessment."

Her fingers lightly massaged the front sides of his neck. He paid no heed to her comment, "A small peri-auricular node on the right."

She peered into his ears and nose with a hand-held light, which she then turned on his throat. He fretted that she was intent on exploring every orifice; but for the rest of the exam, he withdrew into the comfort of being touched.

"You still haven't looked at my wound," he asserted when she returned to the desk and recorded her findings.

"I'm afraid to," she answered with the EKG at hand. "It looks like you haven't changed the dressing."

"Once, actually. I removed it to take a look, but I didn't have any bandages to replace it."

"How did it happen?" With gloved hands, she cut the bandage. "This is going to hurt," she warned but did not delay.

"Whoa!" he shouted as the flash of her hand ripped away the encrusted bandage. "I thought a woman's touch would be gentler!"

"Sometimes an artist has to do what is most expedient," she snickered while unraveling the remainder of the bandage.

"Between you and Mrs. Wright, I don't think I'm going to get any sympathy."

"Oscar Wilde suggested that the less said of life's tribulations, the better. Rather, one should sympathize with the color, the beauty, and the joy of life. I say '*Cry watercolors*'." She evaluated the wound and concluded, "It actually looks pretty good."

"*Cry watercolors*," he repeated quietly, but then asked

Dr. Revels, "To master a human complexity through a metaphor... Do you think that would make a poetic riddle easier to solve?"

"Poetic riddles and the human condition," she answered. After applying a new bandage, she then added matter-of-factly, "Keep it clean, and change the bandage daily."

The doctor finished her review at her desk.

After redressing, he asked, "Well, Doc, how long do I have to live?"

"Well, your exam was unrevealing, except for that neck node we'll just need to re-evaluate on your return visit. We'll also discuss the laboratory results." She grabbed the EKG from the clipboard and, with a serious stare, she added, "But the tracings of your EKG suggest a recent heartbreak."

"You're kidding. An EKG can tell you that?"

"Why not? If a fortune teller can judge the spirit of a man from tea leaves, palms, and tarot cards, I should think the tracings of a man's heart would be much more accurate." She chuckled. "That, my friend, is the art of medicine."

"And I was beginning to trust you."

"But seriously," she continued, "you should consider mid-life as a new beginning. It's an opportunity to take knowledge from your past and follow the wisdom of your heart, rather than the passion of your mind. Metaphorically: To cry watercolors and enjoy the composition."

"Are those your closing remarks on every mid-life physical?"

"No, just for guys that Kathleen taunts into pulling at their wrinkles."

Dr. Revels waited at the door, as if for further discussion, but Mark remained silent. "I wish you good fortune," she added and stepped out of the room.

Chapter 14

The interlaced fibers of a spider's snare were tethered to his hiking boots. Desiccated insects decayed in its trap. A butterfly wing jutted from it—a still life of flight. Spiders spin their web in man's indifference.

Mark sat in the garage on a storage shelf, pondering the spider's web. Its intricacy, he thought, was in the simplicity by which each fiber was interwoven about the other. The miracle was in the spider's fulfillment of function: to trap its prey.

He reached for the boots, as if to an estranged appendage, and wished he had worn them on the hike through the peninsular park at Lake Tahoe. Instead, because of neglect, generations of spiders had been sheltered within the leather boots. He plucked the butterfly wing from its bed, but the cobweb he left intact: the boots were the spider's rightful claim.

At eye level, he held the wing with two fingers and noticed black outlining the veins that once supplied its nutrients, but now only traversed an amber field. It was the composition of the wing that, even in its demise, remained beautiful.

"*Cry watercolors,*" Mark recited to himself in the tone of divulging a new-found principle: focus life on the composition, not its tribulations. With that understanding, he ached to be with Emilia.

◆ ◆ ◆

"Arren Sheffer's office, this is Betty. May I help you?"

"You have already," he said into the phone.

"Mark, I was just thinking about you! I had a very good time last night. I hope I didn't ramble on too much."

"Not at all… Matter of fact, that's why I called." He raised the butterfly wing he was still pinching between two fingers. "I'm doing what you suggested: I'm going back to the Lake to ask the poet directly." Though he had no plans, he intended for the composition to unravel on his journey.

"There's no other way," she replied. "You have to find out what could become, rather than bemoan what could have been… I'm really happy for you."

"Is Arren in?"

"So, it wasn't me you're calling for?" Betty quipped.

"Truth be told, I would rather talk to you all day; but since Arren is our boss, I should give him some attention."

"Arren had advised me to be patient, that you were just shy," she laughed. "But in fact, you're truly sly as a fox."

"Hopefully I am and can successfully resolve the riddle."

"Hold on," she said. "I'll transfer you."

"Mark, good to hear from you," Arren said. "Betty told me you two went out to dinner last night. How was it? Isn't she a great gal?"

"That she is. We had a good conversation." He hesitated before adding, "I'll be going out of town for a while."

"What do you mean? How long is a while?"

"I'll be at Lake Tahoe, but I'm not sure for how long." He stared at the wing. "I have a life to make up for."

"Oh, geez, Mark. Did you kill someone?"

"What are you talking about?" *Maybe myself*, he thought.

"Running away to make up for a life... If that's not cryptic for having murdered someone—" Arren began.

"Arren, you've been editing crime articles too long. I'm just going to do what you suggested—remove my blinders."

"It's a mid-life crisis, Mark. All men go through it. You don't have to go off the deep end." Arren sounded hurried as if to stop a train. "Wait a minute. This is about a chick, right?"

"Well, not one that hatches."

"Oh, God... How am I going to break it to Betty? She really is a good woman."

"I know she is. Just tell her I went for a poetry lesson."

"What kind of lame-brain excuse is that?" Arren shouted into the phone.

"She'll understand."

"Oh, geez, Mark... All right, all right, after forty-one years of marriage, I'll think of a better excuse. Now, how about your article?"

"I'll fax you the latest one. But Arren, it's different than anything I've written in the past."

"Ah, shit! Okay, okay, I'll judge later. Just get it to me."

"I'm sure it'll work out," Mark said it more for himself than to assure Arren. "I'll keep you posted on other articles."

◆ ◆ ◆

The winter lawn crinkled under each step he took when crossing the front yard. Mark glanced over the neighborhood and realized his lawn was the only one colored mustard from neglect. He planned to arrange for a gardener while he was gone.

With plenty of sun shining, it was difficult to heed the reports of rain for later in the evening. He hoped it would not snow in the Sierras, at least until he reached Lake Tahoe.

At Fredricksons' front door, the doorbell rang three times before Mark heard a latch slide open. In the gap of the partly-opened door, the cop's wife stood guarding it, with one foot wedged behind it.

"Can I help you?" she asked.

"Hi. Sorry to bother you. I'm Mark, your next-door neighbor." He pointed towards his home. "I'll be out of town for about two weeks, and I was hoping you would keep an eye on the house while I was away."

"Oh, yes. I'm sorry I didn't recognize you." Her hand let go of the inside handle and combed back her hair. The door was opened wider. "We don't see much of you."

"I'm pretty much a recluse. I suppose many writers are."

"So, you're a writer? Interesting," she said with a tone of wanting to pry further. "My husband is a cop, but you know that. We'll certainly keep a watch." She turned her face to the cry of a newborn from inside her home. She grasped the casing of the door. "I'm Rose, and that's my four-week-old Andrew you hear calling. He's just as demanding as his dad."

"Congratulations on the baby, and I won't keep you any longer. Thanks for watching the house."

"No problem. I'm glad we finally got to meet. Maybe

we can have you over when you return." She held the edge of the door and motioned to close it.

"That'd be nice," he said as the door was shut.

Later in the evening, voices of children parried their parents' summons, until the last one at play was called the harshest. He listened as the children's sounds faded into the chirp of a cricket.

◆◆◆

Two large garment bags were set by the door, bulging with as much as he could pack. The hiking boots he let remain where the spiders had claimed them.

From one of the pants stuffed into the luggage he withdrew the doctor's reminder for the next appointment, but discarded it with the rest of the rubbish.

Emilia's note remained safeguarded in the breast pocket of his shirt but crinkled loudly in the grip of his hand. Mark re-read the flare in her writing, which invited him to call.

As if with the deliverance granted a man from death watch, Mark faxed Sadie's tale. With it, he attached a note for Betty that reported, *I've gone for a poetry lesson.*

Chapter 15

The *geometry-of-emotion* is the distance between a volatile point and fulfillment. In Mark's state of mind, the highway was the quickest route between these two points.

A spray of mist from the slower cars was all that remained of the earlier rainfall. Ahead of him, on route to Lake Tahoe, was a pale blue sky he hoped would overtake the smoke-gray clouds that lingered at the eastern ridge of the Sierras.

As rivulets of rainwater cascaded in the gullies on the side of the road, lightning flashed in the ridges as he ascended the mountain to his home. As if in a deluge, rainfall fell behind him just as he shut the front door.

From the frenzy of the weather to the agitation of his nerves, Mark found no respite being indoors. He rushed to the phone and, from the crinkled paper Emilia had invited him to call, dialed her number.

"...leave a message," is all he heard the monotone voice request, but he could not muster a voice to respond.

On a second attempt, he was unable to group words for a petition, nor contrition, to be with her again. "Hi... this is Mark," is all he was able to claim.

A man obsessed is one without much else to do, but

the activity he manipulated to distract his thoughts only magnified his impatience. With a burst of energy, he snatched the keys from the kitchen counter and drove off into town.

Mark slowed the storm door from slamming as he quietly entered the Maidu Café. From behind the wet jacket he hung on the coat-rack he glanced into the dining room and noticed it appeared empty. He slipped into the counter's first seat.

"Hi. Would you like a menu?" a young waitress asked and placed a glass of water with the silverware.

"Yes, please." He did not recognize her, nor the name on her tag. "Karen. Hmm… You must be new."

"No, not really. I've been here for ten months, ever since I graduated from high school." She wiped the counter. "I mostly work the afternoon shift."

She was lean and tall, much as expected of a skier. Her black hair was plaited in a single braid from the back of her head and hung to her waist. From the service window she picked up a tray and carried the meal to the diner he had missed on the first inspection.

Victor was at a table by the back window and appeared to have been startled by Karen's arrival. His thoughtful glance quickly transformed into a smile, and they became engaged in conversation. Her responding giggle seemed to propel her back to the counter.

"Ready to order?" she asked Mark.

"I'm sorry. Let me look at your specials." He hesitated, but as she turned away, he quickly added, "Is Emilia working today?"

"No," Karen answered from the wash basin, where she poured out the old coffee from a glass urn. "I believe she's out of town."

"Oh, I see." He glanced at Victor, who pensively

stared at the rain. Mark took a sip of water as if to squelch a thought. "Do you know where she went?" he asked Karen.

"No, but I'm sure she'll be here tomorrow." She replaced the urn on a metal burner and walked into the kitchen. Coffee began to drip into the pot.

Tomorrow, he thought, *was a cheap overture to hope,* but he gladly accepted it rather than be further tormented with impatience. A flash of light from outside the front window heralded the loud crash of thunder. Mark hoped the storm would quickly pass before Emilia's safe return.

◆◆◆

"How are you, Victor?" Mark asked, having approached from the restroom.

Victor looked up from his stare out the window and replied with a question, "Hey, guy. What's up?"

"We met at Steamers," Mark answered. "I came with Emilia."

"Emilia came with Norma," he corrected. "Didn't she?"

"That's right. Emilia invited me to meet the group."

"Yeah, I remember you." Victor took a bite of the sandwich. "She's a fine lady. Always kind to stray cats."

And dirty dogs, Mark wanted to counter.

"I suppose you're here to see her, too."

"Karen says she's out of town."

"Yeah, man. Hey, sit down." Victor pointed to the seat across from him. "She goes to Berkeley for some religious thing."

"That's right; she mentioned that." Mark sat down. "Native American prayers."

"I guess it was a good day to get out of town. This weather sucks." Victor glanced out the window.

"Thought you left." Karen approached their table. "Ready to order?" she asked Mark.

"I think I'll just have a diet coke," he answered.

"How about you, Victor?" she asked. "Anything else you want?"

"No, thanks," he replied. "You're all I can handle!"

Karen giggled on her return to behind the counter.

"She's a great kid," Victor added, "but she's also my boss's daughter. Totally out of bounds for me." He sipped his drink and glanced in her direction. "She sure filled in nicely, though."

On her return, Karen winked at Victor when setting Mark's drink on the table. "The Rodeo Dance is at the Elks Club on Friday," she said to Victor.

"Can't wait to see you in them tight jeans!" Victor replied.

"They're yours when you want 'em!" The swivel of her hips seemed exaggerated on her return to the counter.

"Ride 'em, cowgirl!" Victor whooped in response.

"*Out-of-bounds* seems to have no limitations," Mark said.

"It's just horseplay. But hell," he said with a wink to Mark, "you got to keep a woman moistened. You never know when you'll need a ride!"

"And I suppose you keep the spurs at the ready?"

"I never seem to take 'em off!" He leaned forward and dropped his arms to his lap, then added, "And you gotta keep *the gun* always loaded!"

Forethought seems to be as titillating as foreplay, Mark thought, *and Betty would probably consider it a variant of sexual self-sufficiency?* He mentally snickered on thinking how one's sexual prowess can become engorged through imagination.

"Aren't you tired?" Mark asked. "Always having to be ready?"

"On a day like today? Sure." Victor slumped back on his chair. "Today I've nothin' to do but horseplay with a high-school kid."

"Why not settle for one woman?"

"I would consider settling down for Emilia. She's a fine woman, but she says I lack graces." As his face became contorted with laughter, he looked up at Mark. "I guess she didn't like me burpin' at the table!"

"No... I wouldn't think she would." Mark's restrained laugh sounded more of a snigger until he managed to ask more soberly, "What do you think she meant by that...? Ah, forget it. It doesn't matter."

"Women are like that. They play along with your jokes and tolerate your gases, but when they want something that you can't guess at, they blame your graces." Victor's preaching sputtered into finger-pointing snicker. "Don't tell me she got you with it, too? What did you do, come with the wind and leave with a fart?" He snorted through his nose and tears gathered in the corners of his eyes.

Mark thought it would be conspiratorial to reciprocate the laugh and a betrayal to continue with the joke. He, though, wondered why Emilia considered Victor a friend she still defended. Mark fought the urge to stand up and walk away; but instead, he watched the contortions of Victor's handsome features reveal the loneliness he worked to hide.

Chapter 16

Like a swarm of locusts on the shingles of his roof, rain continued to fall. As if drawn into a trance, Mark stared out the picture window in the living room and watched the sunlight gradually re-emerge over the panorama of the lake. The departing rain settled into a comforting silence.

"Hello, Emilia," he spoke to the voicemail message and returned the crinkled paper to his shirt-pocket. "I've called to apologize, but I know there's no forgiveness for what I did." He hoped his deep sighs were not recorded and then added, "Call me when you get back."

◆ ◆ ◆

It sounded like the clamor of thunder awakening him, but the second ring led his hand to the phone.

"Hello." He worked alertness from his nap.

"I hope I didn't wake you."

Jolted by her voice, he sat up to the edge of the bed. "Emilia!" he exclaimed. "It's okay. I was hoping you'd call."

"It's good to hear from you. I just got your message."

"I'm so glad you called me," he said. "Are you home?"

"Yes, I just got in. I was in Berkeley for the last three days. I had to wait out the rain."

"I'm glad you waited. It was a bad storm."

"Are you all right?" she asked.

"Me? Yes, of course. I've been indoors all day. Are you?"

"I'm pretty tired from the drive, and I've got to get to bed for a few hours of sleep before going in to work."

"I've been worried about you driving in the rain," he said, but it was not the topic he wished to dwell on. He cleared his throat as if inside a confessional and stared at an imagined purple shroud of Lent, taunting him to uphold his penance of solitude. "I'm sorry," Mark said in a raised voice as if to rip apart the purple shroud. "Like a coward... I left you even when I wanted you most."

"I want to see you, Mark. I've—"

"I know you're tired," he quickly interjected. "You have to get some rest before getting to work... How about I invite you for dinner after work?"

"I'd love that! After all, my cupboards are totally bare."

"Great. Then it all works out." He hung up the phone, but in his mind, he cataloged Disney characters Emilia was unlikely to eat. He fell asleep without deciding on what meat to serve.

◆ ◆ ◆

The following morning, Mark began to prepare for the meal, but slammed the cooking book closed on recalling that recipes only thwarted his pursuit of adventure. With his favorite recipe requiring a dash of this or that, added to whatever was in the refrigerator, he thought it best to get his empty cupboards better stocked.

As if at the epicenter, Maidu Café seemed to be just down the street from everywhere he traveled. On the way to the market, he could not help but notice the parking lot was not crowded.

Only three tables were occupied, and one diner sat at the counter. Emilia's back was turned to him as she stood at the service window, waiting for an order. As if propelled by a sudden surge of palpitations, he stepped in from the foyer but did not stop the door from shutting behind him. Emilia turned to the loud thump of the door.

"Mark!" she shouted but froze where she stood.

At the counter, he reached over it to embrace her with a kiss. "I'm sorry," he said on the need for a breath. "I had to stop and see you."

She wiped her lipstick off his face. "I'm so glad you did!"

"Order up!" the cook shouted from the kitchen.

"The breakfast is gonna get *cold!*" Laura cautioned on her pass behind Emilia.

"Stay here and have a seat," Emilia said to Mark, retrieving the plates at the service window.

"I'm holding you up," he said on her pass to the couple at the front table. "I better get going."

"Let me get you breakfast!" she offered on reaching for condiments from under the counter.

"I'm full right now, since all I've been thinking of is what to prepare for you tonight. I was actually on my way to the market."

"Then let me walk you to the car." She reached back to untie her apron. "Laura, I'm just stepping out for a second."

"Don't worry. You're busy," he backed away from his counter seat. "I don't want Laura to have a bad impression of me."

"She doesn't care where I go, as long as it's with a man… All right, I won't keep you, but tell me what we're having for dinner."

"Moroccan road-kill and Loch Ness eel."

She pulled back as if from a sting. "Interesting, but not very romantic!"

He reached for her hand to kiss. "It's all I could come up with that Disney has not made a movie of." He walked backward to the door. "I've missed you."

Inside the market, he imagined himself in an enchanted land, soaring on a magic carpet into a Marrakech bazaar. The smells were of exotic spices, and the produce was captivating in its vibrant colors. Wanting to share his fairy-tale adventure, he planned to arrange the items of the meal into a colorful array.

Later that night, the living room pendulum-clock chimed on the half hour before Emilia was to arrive. Mark rushed to get the final preparations done. Looking over the disarray in the kitchen, his doctor's warning came to mind: *to cry watercolors and enjoy the composition.* On that night, it was only the palette he worried about.

Startled by the doorbell, he quickly closed the oven to keep warm the garlic chicken. Taking a second look through the oven door he was satisfied that the meal, wrapped with bacon strips and garnished with colorful vegetables, looked delicious.

"Welcome to my front row center on Paradise," he said on opening the door. "Dinner will soon be served."

Emilia handed him an armful of red roses and a boxed chocolate cake. "I'm hoping you didn't get to make dessert," she said.

"You brought everything I forgot to get," he replied. "I've never been given flowers before." He clasped the roses at their stems and held them bundled upside down; the boxed-cake he pressed gently to his chest. "Thank you so much. I hope the meal will complement them." He leaned to her for a kiss.

"We need to work on transcending *never*," she replied and embraced him in a kiss.

"If I'm likewise rewarded," he said and licked his lips, "there's nothing I won't hesitate to transcend."

In the living room, Emilia removed her coat. "Mmm! Smells delicious!"

"Everything is ready!" Mark said from behind her.

She turned to the darkened kitchen and switched the light on, "Goodness!" she said to the disarray revealed. With a swift hand, she took back the cake box and added, "You better put those roses in water before you crush them."

Mark inhaled the fragrance from the roses as if for encouragement, then placed them into a flask that he then set on the coffee table in the living room.

"Mark!" she said from the kitchen. "I didn't mean for you to kill them! They need water!"

He returned to the kitchen with the flask and noticed Emilia's flower print dress complemented the roses he carried. "You look beautiful," he said.

She had placed the cake on a serving crystal he was surprised he owned. She raised the lid from over the chicken, and a flush of steam rose from it. "Mmm… It smells delicious."

"And does being delicious make you want more?" He handed her the flask.

"Of course it does… especially since I'm starving." She filled the flask with water and set it on the peninsula bar separating the dining area. With a flare in hand motion, she arranged the roses.

"I could never have done it so beautifully," he said and counted the roses. "Why seven?"

"A dozen is a ritual," she answered while carrying the arrangement to the dining table, "and a single rose is a cliché. Whereas, half a dozen is only a wish... Ah, but *seven* is a promise!"

"You're so rich with puzzles," he said, staring at the flowers. "You give substance to what otherwise would be trivial... So, tell me—a promise of what?"

"To give you more." Emilia turned to him and lightly touched the side of his face.

Mark took a deep breath and listened to the chime from the living room. And if the span of the clock's arms dutifully created time, he wished for the chime to be silenced at that moment.

"Your puzzles may not make you an oracle," he said, "but to me, they make you a fairy... a Cherokee fairy. Everything you do and say fascinates me."

"I'm just a simple waitress," she said on her turn back to the kitchen, "and so, I will serve the dinner."

"No, no!" He held her hand to stop her return. "Let *me* try to charm *you*, for at least half as much as you have done me." He pulled a chair for her to sit. "I don't want you to think of me only as the guy with egg yolk on his shirt."

"I could get used to being pampered," she replied, sitting.

"Knowing how important grace is for you, I'll do it all to music. What kind would you like me to put on?"

"How about some country-western?" she answered.

"Good, because I broke the antenna of my ghetto blaster, and that's all I get up here." Mark worked the tuning of the radio in the living room.

"No worries," she said. "I love the melodrama of regular folk set to music."

'Desperado' played in the background as Mark set the table with the meal. "This song is about me," he said, matter-of-factly.

"Is that Clint Black singing it?" Emilia asked. "What about the song is you?"

"I'm the 'Desperado'—*sitting on the fences, unable to come to my senses.*"

"I don't understand," she replied.

He returned with a bottle of Chardonnay. "Would you like some wine?"

She raised her glass to let him pour but remained silent, as if expecting a revelation.

Mark took the seat beside her and poured wine into his glass. He remained quiet, struggling with the words crossing his thoughts. As if for a pronouncement, he hastily stood and raised his glass. "To *cry watercolors...* and enjoying the composition."

Emilia clinked her glass to his, and they both took a sip. "I suppose I'm not the only one with puzzles," she said with a quizzical stare toward him.

"It's like the song suggests: *It may be rainin', but there's a rainbow above you...* My doctor's metaphor is Cry Watercolors, by which she means not getting caught up on life's hardships; but rather, to focus on its composition." He continued serving the meal.

"The song also talks about coming to your senses and letting someone love you before it's too late. Would that be more of what your doctor was referring to?" she suggested.

"It's why I returned... to ask you for a second chance." Mark returned her gaze and reached for her hand.

"It's not that I wasn't hurt," she said, "or that I understood why you left, but I hoped you would return. There's no second chance… I never did let go of what we were creating."

Mark felt the softness of her hand and outlined the glossy art on her fingernails. He stared at the base of each finger that was absent of any ring shadows. He traced the contour of her veins and embraced their course to her heart. He leaned to her, and she to him, and with their kiss, he promised to overcome the limits of *never*.

On the balcony after dinner, Emilia tightened the afghan wrap around her shoulders and reclined on the chaise lounge chair. Pensively, she stared at the black sky and waited for Mark to sit. "It's an incredible view from here," she said.

"It's even more spectacular in daylight."

"It's magnificent how black and endless everything appears," she said and stood up to the banister.

Mark stared from his lounge chair in her direction. Only black shadows were discernible. Except for themselves and the shimmer of stars, the universe was a void. He looked up to where the constellations, much like flakes in a snowstorm, seemed to spiral into an abyss. At the railing, Emilia appeared to be among them.

The silence beyond their voices stalked the rustle of a gentle breeze among the trees. Were it not for the flicker of lights on the south shore, he could imagine they were alone on earth.

"There are a billion stars in that sky," she said.

"Can you be sure of that?" he replied.

"Yes," she said, and with a finger dipped into the void, she began to count. "There's Taurus and Orion. Ah, let's see how many other constellations I can make out."

"When did you study the constellations?"

"When I told fortunes." Emilia turned, but in the darkness, she followed only his voice.

"You were a fortune teller?" he asked in disbelief.

"Not really. But in my religious studies, I attempted to apply Greek philosophical corollaries of the zodiac to contemporary events." She set herself on Mark's lounge chair, and he dropped his legs to either side and made her room.

"Whatever that means," he replied. "It sounds much more complicated than fortune telling." He wrapped his arms around her.

"It only means I spent a lot of time studying but proved nothing."

She rested against his chest. "Your hands are freezing." She raised the afghan and cast it around them both.

"That feels so much better," he said. "What do you think of fortune telling? Is there anything to it?" He remembered the doctor reading his fortune from an electrocardiogram.

"The Greeks, as well as many other ancient cultures, believed that human pathos interplay with the constellations. But I believe we are the product of our *will* interacting with the environment. One question difficult to answer is the importance of destiny—and whether this is godliness…" She turned her head and glanced at him. "I'm not a fatalist, so fortune telling is more of *wishing* than *willing*."

"How about our chance meeting?" Mark kissed her forehead. "Was it our destiny, or my willing it?"

"To be honest, it was my diehard patience!" she laughed.

"What do you mean?"

"It took you so long to acknowledge my interest!"

"That's what you would call *sitting on the fence*," Mark replied soberly, but then added, "You know, my doctor actually read my fortune from an EKG."

"Well, why not? it should be a more direct measure than tea leaves." She turned to look back at the darkness.

"That's exactly what she said."

"And what was your fortune your doctor read?" she asked.

"She actually went through a ritual before reading the EKG, but I'll spare you those gory particulars. Through my electrical energies, she assessed my need to seek out the wisdom of my heart, more so than the passion of the mind."

"Interesting concept," she said.

"But for you, I need both wisdoms: my heart and mind are equally fascinated by you."

Emilia let the afghan fall from her grip and turned to him, "*Desperado*, let me love you before it's too late."

Mark carried Emilia, snugly cradled in his arms. Passing the radio, he flitted with his feet to the rhythm of the music. Down the stairs, he teetered with her weight. Laying her on his bed, he felt the surge he recalled only from his high school days.

Emilia spoke upon his lips, "Be still... Let me make love to you tonight." Her breath was inside him, and he wished never to exhale.

The window blinds remained open, but in the darkness, only the forest was their witness. Without sight, he touched the beauty of her flesh.

"Shh," she appealed when he whispered his desire to reciprocate. Motionless, he succumbed to a storm of pleasure.

Chapter 17

Green ponderosa pine needles dazzled in the reflected morning sunlight. A blue jay assumed a perch on the roughened wood of the deck. Patches of snow remained only on the shadowed craggy hillside of the forest. Staring out from his bed, Mark realized his life had changed as quickly as winter had become spring.

Emilia still slept on his arm as he watched her eyelids flutter. His fingers skimmed her naked flesh and brushed the curls of her hair, unfurled on the pillow. Her perfume was the scent of the flowers she had worn. He remained motionless under the quilted comforter, afraid to awaken her.

"Good morning," he said when he noticed her eyes squint against the light.

"Good morning," she answered and rubbed her eyes to gain a focus. "Have you been awake long?"

"I don't know about being awake, but certainly dreaming," he replied.

She raised herself partly over him. "I know a better way to find out if you're awake or dreaming."

"Better than a pinch…" he asked but was silenced

with her lips on his.

"You're right," he said when she dropped to his side, "Dreams don't taste as good."

"Talking of taste, I can make us breakfast," she offered. "Karen switched with me for this morning. I won't have to go in 'til early afternoon." Emilia rested her head on his chest. "You know I wanted last night to happen."

"So did I." He combed his fingers through her hair. "Thank you for being patient."

In the downstairs bedroom, the clock's chime was not audible, but even so, Mark was aware time continued to pass on—the sun lifted shadows into their room.

"I suppose I better get ready and make you breakfast." She cast off the comforter before Mark replied, then moved away from the bed toward the bathroom. "Would you like to join me?" she asked from the door. He remained in the bed to watch her prepare.

"The water feels great," she shouted from the shower: he ran to her.

◆ ◆ ◆

Summits along the mountain range seemed like spires of ancient cathedrals, rising above the mist that shadowed the lake at the shore. It was late morning when they sat at the table for breakfast.

"Two eggs, over easy, home fries, two whole-wheat toasts, and a cup of coffee." She set the meal before Mark. "Did I forget something?"

"No, you've got it all."

"Mark Balcon." She sat at the table and poured milk into her bowl of cereal. "You are a man of habit."

"And what have you thought about that?" he asked and dipped the toast into the yolk.

"About what?" she asked.

"My being a man of habit."

"We pattern our lives for comfort when we are most afraid of its challenges."

"Is that what you see in me?" He placed the fork back on the table and looked at her.

"I've seen so much, and yet so little of who you are; but what I've seen has led me here." She reached for his hand. "For two years, I've thought about this moment."

"Don't you think it's sad to hide from life's challenges?" He picked with the fork at the toast as if for something hidden. "To forever sit on the fence... Was it pity that kept you interested?"

Emilia sat back and stared out the window. "Look at all the beautiful things around us, and most often we simply admire them for how beautiful they appear to be." She continued, "But our lives would be so much richer if we pursued the curiosity these provoked... If our time together had not happened, if I had not touched you nor cooked your breakfast, my knowing you would be limited to what I had judged you to be." She smiled at Mark and added, "I would only know your eccentricities."

He scooped a forkful of egg and bit into it. "Well, as long as it's not me you pity," he said and wiped the drip of yolk from the corner of his mouth.

As if to quell their laughter, the water kettle whined with a shrill cry. "I thought I turned it off," Emilia said on her way to the kitchen. "Would you like more coffee?"

"You know," he answered, "in my former solitude, the kettle's whine was company." He gazed at Emilia when she returned. "Now it's just a nuisance."

"Let's plan on keeping it that way." She glanced at

the panorama as if to a sundial. "Oh, my word! I'm going to be late!"

She rushed to gather her coat and purse but stopped at the front door. "This is the first time Karen let me switch, so I better not discourage her from doing it again." She reached for him one step behind her. "That kettle better never have anything over me!" She kissed him before stepping out toward her truck.

Mark felt a shiver with the cool breeze but waited to watch her truck make the last turn at the bottom of the hill. Inside, he cleared the dining table and reset the flower flask on it. The bouquet appeared to have bloomed—the cluster of petals had broadened since the night.

One petal fell and brushed his hand as he wiped around the flask. He recalled her proverb: seven roses, one more than a wish, but plenty of promises before it would be a ritual... *Fragile promises?* he wondered, as petals continued to drop with each swipe. He quickly withdrew his hand.

◆◆◆

He sat by the picture window, attempting to work on an article. Distracted by a soft thump, he scurried to the side window from where the sound had come. Looking out, he noticed moisture stains on the splintered wooden deck, remnants of an icicle's silent cascade.

Outside, on the floor below the window, he found a bird turned on its side. It formed shallow breaths in an apparent struggle for its life. In the cup of Mark's hand, the dark-eyed Oregon junco was hooded with black feathers, but its head remained still. Only its somber eyes seemed to express an appeal. The charcoal wings, edged with white, were drawn against its body, and the legs were flexed as if stilled in flight. It remained unmoving until a cough of blood preceded a wild flap of the wings; its breath ceased thereafter.

We pattern our lives for comfort when we are most afraid of its challenges, he recalled Emilia's words.

And nature enriches all living things with the challenges it bestows, he mindfully replied.

The hill sloped down at the side of the house. At the base of a Jeffrey pine tree, Mark dug a shallow grave into the rocky ground and covered the entombed bird with loose dirt and gravel.

As if with a bishop's crown, a blue jay proudly sat on a nearby boulder and twittered a scolding that Mark imagined was a burial rite.

Look at all the beautiful things around us, Emilia had advised, and he was lured by his curiosity to the other sounds beckoning from inside the forest.

Fluorescent moss covered fallen branches, and kindling snapped under his step. In the clearing, seedlings sprouted on the promise of springtime, and among these leaped a Sierra grasshopper, a tenth the size of its cousin. In flight, it sounded as if to chirp with castanets; at rest, it mimicked a dry leaf.

Much like a chickadee, a squirrel's call belatedly warned of the dropped pinecone that fell at Mark's feet. Startled by the sudden sound, he looked back but could not make out the trail he had followed. It made no matter; he continued to the stream he had heard was still deeper within the gorge.

Chapter 18

As Hansel and Gretel did in their fairytale, Mark lost the trail into the forest; but joyfully trekked the flowered rocky walls of the gorge on his return home.

At his front door, the effect of neglect was evident with the frayed varnish of the wood. Skimming its surface with his fingers, he mentally tasked it for immediate sanding—Emilia might get a splinter from it.

Inside the home, only the tick of the clock intermittently broke an unsettling silence. Mark was reminded of when he imagined *Time as an illusion, created in the span of the second's hand and cataloged into memories*. But as he glanced around where Emilia had been, nothing seemed more real than when she dipped her finger among the constellations.

The phone rang and interrupted his musing. "Hello?" he responded on the first ring.

"Mr. Balcon?" He recognized the sonata voice of Dr. Revels' nurse, but not the soberness in her tone.

"Yes," he answered haltingly.

"Dr. Revels has been trying to reach you all day. We called your home and left a message. We finally were able to get in contact with your secretary, who gave us this number." In what sounded like a reprimanding tone, she continued. "Dr. Revels had an emergency at the hospital, but she asked me to set up an appointment for you tomorrow at three."

"Wait a minute!" he said to the storm stirring inside of him. "What does she want me for?"

"She only said that it was important you come in. She didn't say much else." He thought her voice was forgiving, but he wanted it to be apologetic. Her request was intrusive as she continued. "What time would you prefer?"

"I can't come in at all. I'm in Lake Tahoe. It's at least a six-hour drive back." He felt for the wound on his right knee. It was healing well. There was no reason to make the trip. "Just tell her to call me when she returns."

"We need you to come in," Kathleen persisted. "She works a half-day on Saturday. We'll make it for then."

"No!" He wanted to end their quibble. Emilia might want to call before she drove up from work. "I'll talk to Dr. Revels on the phone, and that's all."

"All right," Kathleen said, without a surrender in her voice. "I'll have her call—but you have to come in."

Mark dropped the phone as he would if stung by an electrical spark. *What,* he wondered, *could be the urgency?* His wound was healing well, and he felt better than ever. Besides, Dr. Revels had confirmed his good health.

The nurse had offered a three o'clock appointment, and he recalled the secretary mention they conducted a free clinic about that time. It must be, he decided, that the insurance claim was rejected.

He had left the master bedroom last for housekeeping but smiled at noting its disorder. As his final task, he collected the garments strewn about the room, each seemingly with a tale on how it made its journey. From the glass door opened to the deck, a sweet smell of maple entered with a light breeze.

Later in the evening, from outside on the deck, he listened to the tires of her truck grind the gravel to the front of the home, and then the patter of her steps that quickened to the front door. He rushed upstairs before a second ring.

"I've missed you!" he said on opening the door.

Emilia dropped the clothes she carried and embraced him for a kiss. Her body leaned against his and pressed him to the splintered door. Were it not for a honk of a passing car, he would have preferred to remain at the doorway.

"I suppose this is the right house?" she said and slipped from his embrace to collect her clothes.

"No, I think it's two doors up!" He bent down to help her. "But I don't think the old man would survive your greeting."

"Well, then, you'll just have to do." Wearing the café uniform, Emilia walked past him. "Brought a few things just in case I need a change."

Later, cuddled on the sofa, they faced the idle fireplace. "It's a bit chilly tonight," she said.

Mark removed the decorative shawl hanging from the back cushions of the sofa and wrapped it around her shoulders.

"I was thinking more of firing up the fireplace." She rose to the hearth where a single log was set on a metal grate. "But I think I'll cheat." She turned the valve of a nearby gas spigot and, when the twigs that were overlaid on the log burst into flames, she returned to his side on the sofa.

"I could have done that," he said.

"From the looks of it, you've had that log waiting for

a long while," she replied.

"Procrastination is my middle name."

"Seems that was not the case today," she said. "I kept thinking of you while at work, so I called a few times and only got your voicemail. The last time was just a busy signal."

He held back telling her of the nurse's call that had occupied the phone line. "I'm sorry, but I did as you would have suggested."

"What do you mean?"

"Well... a bird crashed into the window and died. I thought it best to return it to its ancestral land, and so I buried it in the forest. But then I was lured deeper by the sounds of many birds that sang as if for some burial ritual." He smiled at Emilia. "I was in awe of the many beautiful things I saw, and I suppose I stayed out too long."

"Ancestral lands? Seems like I've had some influence," she replied.

"I would say much more than that." He held her hand and kissed her.

"Good," she replied. "Then we shall see the sunrise together."

"Is that a Cherokee proverb?"

"I don't think so. My grandmother told it to me, mostly to cheer me up... I took it to mean that there's no reason to be sad when so much was good."

"Like 'cry watercolors,'" Mark suggested and glimpsed at the phone on the side table. "My doctor used it as an attempt to stop my self-pity in getting older." He hoped the doctor would not be calling.

"To be honest," she interjected, "self-pity can be a method to get some comfort."

"Well, my comfort would be in getting to know more

about you. Why is it that I feel the need to know everything about you?"

"Because a lonely man cries," she answered firmly.

"There you go with another riddle."

"It's not a riddle; just a method to provoke thought for greater insight into the question."

"The Socratic method to educate… All right, but will you explain why a lonely man cries?"

"Would you like it as a doctoral dissertation?"

"Let's keep it simple. Consider your audience."

"OK… when we are hurting, our natural response is to make the pain go away. Therefore, when loneliness is painful, we seek to find company," she replied.

"Seems too clinical," he said. "You are more than an urge to end my loneliness."

"You asked for a simple reasoning. Would you rather I discuss chapter 12 of the dissertation, which is destiny; or chapter 15, which is relevancy and mutualism; maybe chapter 9, which is vulnerability… Better yet, let's forget the dissertation and *see the sunrise together*."

"You're right. But before the sun rises: why do you want me?"

She turned toward Mark. "Because you've invited me to share this moment of our lives."

"If it only takes an invitation—" Mark hesitated for a deep breath. "Why not a man like Victor?"

Mark hoped the chill he felt was of the waning fire. Emilia stood and walked to the fireplace. With a metal poker, she replaced the log in the hearth and stoked the embers until they burst into flames. Back in the sofa, he smelled the balsam fragrance of campfire in her hair.

Of her silence, he wished it was not of detachment; but if he knew anything of Emilia, a retreat was not in her character. He held her hand and waited for a response.

"He told me you met at Maidu," she said.

"Yeah," he answered and pretended composure, but wondered if in his complacency of Victor's mockery, had he transgressed affection of Emilia? Was he guilty of *love without grace*?

"Victor is a wonderful man, but he hides his emotional shortcomings in his physical attributes. With him, there's nothing a good fuck will not heal."

Mark worked to mimic Bullwinkle's demonic grin. "I would've never imagined you using that word."

"It's liberating not to restrict myself to *never*," she replied.

"I want to know everything about you: what you think, what you do, where you're from." His finger swept the curve of her eyes and glided on the slope of her nose. He added, "I'm even jealous of your memories."

"And if lust is the driver, 'it will sate itself,'" she said as if to prompt further inquiry.

"Is that another of your grandmother's proverbs?"

"No, it's from Hamlet—Shakespeare's inference on desiring more beautiful things," she said with an inflection required for a reminder.

"That's right. You did mention before how if one thinks it's beautiful, then one would want more of it."

"I think we're making some progress," she quipped.

"Are your proverbs and allegories mostly influenced by your Cherokee culture?"

"I've never really thought it one way or the other... My goal is to be open to wherever a truth arises." She paused and then added, "Mark, do you see Native Americans through *Hallmark* images?"

"What do you mean?"

"Well, it's not unusual for outsiders to often depict

indigenous cultures through some idyllic poetry, like the four sentence platitudes inscribed on Hallmark postcards."

"Well, then, I can't deny my ignorance. But don't you think sublime ignorance is better than accepting vicious stereotypes?"

"Unmerited innocence, as much as shame, can be equally harmful," she replied. "Every individual deserves the right to transcend *never*, essentially to assert their potential."

"Aside from all the intellectual discussion, I can certainly picture you on a postcard." Mark imagined it being oil stained and hanging in Trapper Garza's coffee shop. "Maybe dressed like an angel and aloft over the clear waters of Lake Tahoe."

"And what would be the platitude you would have printed on it?" she asked.

"Let me think." He recollected phrases from the past.

Inspiration on a half tank of gas,
but a mile up the road
fog obscured the view.

Winding curves ahead
threatened to intercede,
but an angel aloft
set my spirit free.

"That's cute, but not a platitude... Sounds very personal."

"I suppose it describes where I've been heading in my life." She rested her head on his shoulder as he continued, "An old man summed it up for me when he said he had stayed where his folks wanted him to be, rather than go beyond where half a tank of gas would take him: to the lover he had hoped for... But then I came upon you, and now I feel like soaring with you as my angel."

"An angel, maybe, but not angelic," she replied, but her attention seemed to become remote. "William Boatwright would tell you that."

Mark waited for further details, but none followed. "Who is William Boatwright?"

"He was my closest friend in Georgia," her voice became more jovial as she continued, "and my companion in the games we made up from the tales my grandmother told us about the ancient Cherokees who lived in the forest."

"Was he also Cherokee?"

"We thought it didn't matter, but my father called him the *black boy from down the street*," she answered bitterly. "My father didn't know him beyond his skin color."

"I would've thought your father would be more tolerant—coming from a reservation," he said.

"Remember, this was Georgia in the seventies, and my father was an English teacher in a small Christian college. His survival was dependent on adapting by adopting."

"Were you close to your father?"

"My father was terribly distraught after my mother's death and was comforted in self-pity. He withdrew into what he could control, which was his career." She straightened up on the sofa. "My grandmother essentially raised my sister and me."

Emilia held Mark's hand and playfully interlocked her fingers with his. She continued, "In the fourth grade, Billy became my best friend... more so because he enjoyed exploring the forest as much as I did. In there, we would recreate my grandmother's tales."

Hoping to enliven the look on her face, he joked, "It's starting to sound like the makings of a Tom Sawyer story."

"Maybe so, but probably not." The furrows on her forehead seemed to deepen. "Things don't always stay like you wished they would; and a child's game is not so innocent at fifteen. It had been a while since we'd gone into the forest, and I'm not sure why we did on that day, but we got caught in a thunderstorm."

Her deep sighs seemed to accompany painful memories. Mark caressed her, wishing to be where her thoughts were.

"In our soaked clothes, we found shelter in a coyote's den. Pretending to be on watch for the coyote's return, I glimpsed at Billy. With his wet T-shirt clinging to his chest, he appeared more muscular and more attractive than I had ever seen him. I then glanced at myself and feared I was likewise exposed.

"Billy stared away from where I sat, but it appeared as if trying to force his thoughts away from where mine had roamed. We remained silent, but not because we couldn't be heard over the heavy rain or loud thunder.

"In my grandmother's tales, she had warned how a man's eyes lead him to desire; so, I became limp when he turned his gaze on me and trembled when he embraced me. My skin seemed pale against his dark flesh I' clutched. I licked his lips as if their fullness was a magical attribute. The muscles of his body yielded to the thrusts of my wanting him inside me. I envied him in our differences. But when I began to cry, he pulled back and brushed away my tears… what hurt was him stopping."

A spark crackled on what remained of the embers, and dim light from the hall faintly illuminated them on the sofa. Mark realized how much jealousy and self-pity were intertwined. He held her tightly against himself, not so much to comfort her, but as a wish to have been with her then—Mark felt her pain. "What became of Billy?"

"After he walked me home, I never saw Billy again." She hesitated as a tear filled the corner of her eye. "Later that summer, my father rushed to tell me *Billy boy must have gotten himself into trouble.*' There were police and an ambulance when I got down the block to his home." Her voice quivered when she continued. "The following day, I read Billy had gone into the closet and shot himself in the head." Emilia cupped Mark's hand over her lips and kissed the palm. "He never even left a note."

I'm sorry... I'm sorry
Mark said to himself
I'm sorry... I'm sorry
He held her tight
I'm sorry... I'm sorry
Mark also cried.

Chapter 19

Then we shall see the sunrise together, he recalled her grandmother's proverb; but the view from his bed was to the north and into the mountain peaks rising five thousand feet above his home. As much as he tried, he could not detect any of the sunrise colors—at least not without stirring Emilia awake.

A strip of light gradually shone across their entwined bodies, and she awakened when the sunlight fell across her face.

"Good morning," he said.

"Good morning," she answered and stretched her body into his embrace. "I see you didn't run away?"

"Why would I? Actually, I was hoping to catch a view of the sunrise," he said, pointing to the window. "But we're facing the wrong direction."

Prone, she lifted herself onto her bent elbows. "I guess it doesn't matter. You would've had a difficult time waking me at sunrise." She reached for a kiss. "What time is it anyway?"

"By the slant of the shadows, I would say… closer to seven."

She rapidly untangled the comforter from over them, "You're going to get me fired!" She rushed to the bathroom.

"Me?"

"You should've woken me earlier!" The spray from the shower drowned what she then added.

He stood up to the bedside. "You didn't tell me what time you were going in," he said toward her silhouette outlined on the frosted shower glass.

A man's eyes lead him to desire, he remembered her grandmother warn. Mark turned away to the disarray in the room and picked up the comforter, strewn at the foot of the bed.

Outside the shower, she stood naked in front of the mirror and brushed her long black hair. *I envy her for our differences,* he rephrased her words, *but it is why I want her more.*

"I thought you were late," he said, more for her attention.

"Give me some credit!" she laughed. "I told Laura I was going to be an hour late."

"Didn't she wonder why?"

"I told you she doesn't mind if it's because of a man."

"I hope it's not just any man." He hugged her from behind and whispered into her ear, "I want to be the only one with whom you see the sunrise."

Emilia turned to him within his embrace and cradled his face with her hands. She drew him in for a kiss. "There'll be no other," she answered. Stepping back, she asked, "What does that say on your shirt?"

"Orale," he read from his reflection on the mirror. "The accent is on the 'O'. It's an exclamation of pleasure, approval, delight, or victory. Chicano slang for something like 'hurray.'"

"Orale!" she repeated with excitement. "It's like *Cry Watercolors* in Chicano slang."

"You think?" he asked. "I'll make you breakfast

while you finish getting ready."

"Just coffee would be nice. I don't have much time."

A child's game is not so innocent at fifteen, he thought on his way to the kitchen. As he prepared the coffee, he smirked on a thought, *but it sure can be more fun.*

At a corner of the kitchen, the answering machine flashed intermittently with a red light and irked him as if it was issuing a dare. Startled when the kettle loudly shrilled, he marched to the corner and slammed off the flashing light. He would listen to the message later.

My mistress's eyes are nothing like the sun, he murmured to himself, *Coral is far more red than her lips' red.*

"What did you say?" she asked at the top of the stairs.

He quickly turned to her voice, and the hot coffee sloshed in the cup he carried. "Just thinking out loud, on how Shakespeare must have been thinking of you when he wrote that sonnet."

She took the cup. "There's no greater overture of love than poetry."

"So I better get to work on writing a poem for you."

On her return from placing her emptied coffee cup in the sink, he asked, "Can't you call in? Just tell them… tell them you've been kidnapped!"

"It'd be difficult to do that," she said, turning to him at the door, "since I just asked my boss for a week off."

"A week? Just you and me?" He embraced her. "Emilia, that would be fantastic!"

"Here's hoping!" she said, twisting her fingers over each other. "But I'm not sure, on such short notice."

"We'll do anything you want! An entire week together!" His voice was subdued when he added, "I hope I won't bore you."

"My grandmother has a saying—*the chestnut grows best where the tree blooms fall.*"

"I don't understand. Your grandmother will think I'm a fool."

"She simply suggested that what nurtured the tree will nurture the seed. In our case, passion is that nurture. There's no way we could get bored."

"What would she say of a man who'd stayed on the fence for far too long?" he asked, walking her to the car.

"You'll probably be better served taking a note from your friend, Shakespeare, who wrote, *I wear my heart upon my sleeve.*" She hugged him before getting into the car. "It takes no skill to do what you feel, just the courage to know it's right."

He heard the distant sound from inside the house of a garbled voice and then the single sound of an alarm for a received message. He hesitated at the front door to wave farewell as Emilia drove off.

As if transfixed at a railroad crossing, Mark approached the phone and stared at the red flash of a stored message. There was no question it would be Dr. Revels, but Mark did not press the selection to play the recording.

The phone's clamor forced his impulsive hand to reach for the receiver. "Hello?" he asked hesitantly.

"Mark?" a female voice asked. "Did I wake you up?"

"Oh, no, no," he stuttered like a weighted train out of the station.

"This is Betty," she answered. "You couldn't have forgotten us already. Or are you busy?"

"Betty. I'm sorry. My mind was off on another tangent."

"Is everything okay? Arren and I—we've been worried. He said something about you going up there to cover up a murder."

"You're kidding? Ha, ha!" Mark sat down on a nearby chair. "He didn't really say that, did he?"

"He was only joking, but I can tell he's worried."

"I'm here to reclaim my life," he asserted, "and I'm doing as you recommended. I'm here to get answers directly from the poet… but I'm glad you called. How's everything in the publishing business?"

"We're still using ink to get the message out. Mark, it hasn't been that long for anything to have changed," she replied. "Arren did love your short story, but he's already worrying about the next one. Leave it to him to worry about something. By the way, your doctor's office called yesterday. The nurse said they had to get a hold of you right away. I gave them your number." With a more sober voice, she added, "Have you any idea what it's about?"

"Gee, Betty. You sound like you expect them to give me a death sentence. It's more probable the insurance forms didn't go through." He glanced at the red flash.

"Yeah, that's probably true. I suppose the doctor would consider it a death sentence if he didn't get his money. Would they take a kidney back if you didn't pay for the transplant?" Betty chuckled. "I better get going. Arren will dock me for being late. Let me know how it goes with the poet and the doctor."

"I sure will. And thanks, Betty, for caring. Oh, and tell Arren the body has decomposed and is now in the trunk… of *his* car."

"Oh, he'll love that!" she said and hung up.

With his stare fixed as if on the railroad crossing-light, and the dial tone bellowing into his ear, Mark held the phone with a tight grip. Betty's concern, though, prodded him to press the numbers.

"Internal Medicine," responded a voice on the other end.

"Dr. Revels, please." He tried to soften his voice from sounding as if making a demand.

"Who's calling?"

He recalled the secretary's name. "Nancy, this is Mark Balcon. I'm only returning her call."

"Yes, please hold," Nancy directed.

Before the musical tune had carried a single note, another female voice came on the line. "Mr. Balcon? Dr. Revels here. We've been trying to reach you. We need you to come in today."

Had their request been repeated too often, or had he played it in his mind too many times? With irritation, he asked, "Did my insurance not accept the claim?"

"It has nothing to do with your insurance," she replied. "I have to review some of the lab results with you."

"Can we do it over the phone? I won't be able to go in for a while." There was a week of living he was committed to make happen. "I'm in Lake Tahoe, and I can't leave just yet."

"Mr. Balcon—" She accented her requests with formalities. "Some of your results are critical. I can only discuss them with you in person, and it cannot wait."

"It's just going to have to wait until I get back to San Jose."

"When will that be?"

Not until forever, he hoped. "I don't know. One or two weeks, I think."

"Mr. Balcon," she continued, "I wish we had time to wait." Her voice trailed as if into a thought. After a tedious pause, she added, "I took the liberty of having your blood smears reviewed by two pathologists. They both agree that there is a strong probability you have acute myelogenous leukemia."

He heard nothing else the doctor said, but it had to do with further tests and investigations, about doctors to see and treatments to be considered. They were words without feelings, and the only word he could clearly recall was *leukemia*. There was nothing said about his wanting to be with Emilia.

He had promised her to transcend *never*, and to wear his heart on his sleeve. But a trap had been laid: *never* was intertwined with his future. Could one be overcome, he wondered, without severing the other?

On the phone, the doctor tried to explain—only Mark did not want to understand.

The red flash of the railroad crossing sounded an alarm, *But where was the immediacy?* he thought but never asked.

"Let me call you back." He hung up the phone.

Chapter 20

From his writings, and throughout his life, Mark recognized the truth in what Confucius had taught: words are engendered with ideals which their namesakes should be made to follow. But Dr. Revels' words revealed a betrayal that seemingly threatened his life.

He stared into the cold hearth and felt the solitude he knew from before Emilia had ripped it apart. The protection it once had granted, through his control of those ideals bestowed on what he wrote, was now evident to have been a charade. Emilia had left him vulnerable to the passions he had previously distilled onto the characters he wrote about.

The door didn't open, even after a vigorous pull, nor did it respond to a push. Someone's finger, though, rasped on the window and directed his attention to the sign that noted the library did not open until ten o'clock. *It'll only be a thirty-minute wait,* he thought and stepped back a few feet. He continued to stare at the glass door as if to call its bluff.

Stacks of books were visible inside. They seemed like old friends, ready to help his search of a betrayal.

Wind shook the bristles of the pine trees and swept

the cotton fibers of his T-shirt. *Orale*, he thought and supposed Emilia's fingers in the stream of the breeze.

The prick of the stone under his bare feet did not distract his stare as Mark concentrated his imagination on the reflection on the glass door:

> *It appeared like the image of a ghost, all in white. Perched on his head was a black ten-gallon hat; a rattler skin formed the ribbon on the inside of its brim. Readied pistols were holstered at his sides, while eager fingers edged the ivory handles. As he walked the dirt street, his hips carried his feet. He gradually neared, then stopped in a wide stance, recognizing the features of the enemy he knew as "Leukemia."*
>
> *Glacier blue eyes pierced the distance. His hairless face, drawn to a squared chin, bore only the shadow of the hat. His broad shoulders projected beyond the barrels of the pistols. He was hauntingly handsome. As they stood before each other, there was no doubt of their intent. Mark reached for his empty pockets when a metallic bang sounded.*

"Good morning," said the librarian, who flung Mark's foe to the dirt when she swung open the library door. "Isn't it a lovely morning? But aren't you cold?" She gazed at his T-shirt, shorts, and bare feet. He continued, without reply, into the inside.

Rows of shelves were laden with books, radiating from either side of the central lobby. The librarian's counter was just to the side of the entrance. Inside, the hall was bright, lit by the sun, which shone through the large windows on all four walls. Mark was instantly drawn to the reference section, opposite the librarian's counter.

Footsteps that had followed him in dispersed among the other aisles. Mark stood alone among the reference books. He studied their titles and wondered where to begin. There were demographic data, economic statistics, literary annotations... but he was at a loss for medical references.

He couldn't recall if he had ever done such research. The characters he wrote about were more likely to die from common ailments—the bullet inflicted in conflict, and a scorned lover's vengeful stab. His readers would not turn the page unless ahead lay the threat of a cave-in at the silver mines, or an avalanche in the high Sierras. In the Old West he wrote about, no one died of acute myelogenous leukemia. "Or did they?" he asked aloud.

"Did you need some help?" asked the librarian from behind the desk counter, where she shuffled through returned books.

Mark turned toward her. Unless hers was the finger that had rasped the window or the voice that had welcomed him in, he had not noticed her. With hair fastidiously combed, a plain dress buttoned at the collar, and a plaid woolen scarf wrapped about one shoulder, she seemed maternal—a June Cleaver to sort out one's troubles.

"Thank you." He forced a polite monotone, afraid his voice would fail. "Where are your medical references?"

"Let me show you," she said and walked toward him. At the small reference section, she added, "I'm sorry we don't have much in medical references, but I think it'll be a good starting point."

Stowed beyond literary references, and before economic vital statistics, was a small pack of medical books. As she selected a thick paperback, he contemplated the logic for the sequencing of the subjects, but could not think of any.

"This one might have what you're looking for," she said and coaxed the book into his hand. "What, in particular, are you researching?"

Typical wounds in marital discontent, he would have preferred to have said and aroused the librarian's romantic interest. Leukemia would only incite pity. Instead, he blurted, "I'm not sure yet." He balanced the heavy book on the palm of his hand. "But I'm sure I'll find what I need in here."

"If I can be of any help, you know where I'll be." She returned to the counter to shuffle through the stack of books.

At the reading table, he scanned the index of the book. *"Acute myelogenous leukemia,"* he silently read.

Seated at the far end of the table, Mark stared at the words and repeated each for its own merit. "Acute" was innocent, and "leukemia" feminine. These seemed agreeable. "Myelogenous," though, sounded villainous, and if the company these words kept determined character, he decided the doctor's suspicion was evil.

He skimmed through the laborious medical discussion and wondered if a threat existed in an adversary that required only three pages of deliberation. It didn't even have its own chapter. He recognized no personal implications from the reported signs and symptoms and dismissed the thought he was delusional.

The details of its pathology were fogged by medical terms he had to read over to understand. It was a foreign language, but the accompanying English seemed to inflict a growing sense of peril. In untreated cases, there was total fatality; in treated cases, there was a twenty percent cure beyond three years.[1]

He snapped the book shut and threw it to the edge

---

[1] Survival rate for 1999; much progress has been made since

of the table. His eyes moistened as he stared away and realized the consequence of the betrayal.

"Then we'll see the sunrise together," he heard Emilia say in his thoughts. He peered out beyond the window to the crown of trees outside, and listened for her to continue, "No reason to be sad when so much else is good!"

He returned his attention to what he read. There were no alternative treatments presented. Discussed was how to improve the quality of life, its detriment resulting from the treatment's side effects. His thoughts focused on the apparent contradiction.

Should life not be quality? he wondered, and answered the thoughts with recollections of his time with Emilia. He would not allow for a contradiction. Life, he decided, would be quality on its own accord. With a loosely fisted hand, he brushed away a single tear. "I will accept no alternatives," he said.

From the clock on the wall, he counted three hours until Emilia would finish her shift. It was not news he wanted to share, but wanting her in all aspects of what his life would become, it was news he had to tell.

Impulsively, he rose from the table, and the chair screeched loudly on the tiled floor. He turned to the librarian, who responded with a tender smile to his grimace of apology. The book sounded hollow when he pressed it back into the shelf.

"Did you find everything you needed?" she asked as he marched by her counter toward the door.

"Yes, thank you very much," he answered with a wave of his hand.

The metal clanged when the door closed behind him. He turned back to the library door and noticed the reflection of his menace had vanished from the glass.

All he could recall of his drive to the beach was the moment he opened the truck door at the waterfront park. Barefooted, he strolled along the water's edge as frigid alpine water lapped at his feet. He sat on the warm sand and listened to a breeze propel the gentle waves. It was a good spot, he thought, to wait until Emilia would be finished at work.

A throat-clearing sound startled him awake. He shielded his eyes from the bright sunlight but remained still within his imprint on the sand, formed while he napped.

"Excuse me, sir," a masculine voice announced from beyond his field of vision. "I noticed you lay still for a long while. Just wanted to make sure you're OK."

Mark bolted up and turned to the voice. A forest ranger stood a few feet away. "Sorry... I guess I fell asleep." He recognized the face. "You're the guy at the gym," he exclaimed.

"And the ranger on this beach," he replied with an apparent attempt to maintain a solemn tone.

"I don't think I was breaking any rules by napping—was I?" Mark noticed a sting on the flesh of his chest. "I guess I've been asleep for a bit, at least long enough to get a sunburn... I'm Mark," he said and walked to the picnic table the ranger sat on.

"I'm Shannon," the ranger responded. "Was it love problems that brought you out here?"

"Why would you think so?"

"Only lovers seem to do foolish things," Shannon said.

"Like baring their chest for a long nap under the sun?" Mark took a seat across from Shannon.

"Maybe that, but more so, your look of worried

anticipation," Shannon replied. "Your thoughts wear heavily on your face... I can almost see her."

"If you can, you would have amazing skills of observation," Mark replied, feeling a blush on his cheeks.

"Comes from watching over *Yogi Bear*," Shannon answered.

"You might be right in my case." To judge a man's sensitivity was not a skill Mark trusted of himself, but he acted on it for that moment. "You may know her— Emilia Nahhula."

"Emilia, the waitress at Maidu?" That Shannon replied with a question annoyed Mark.

"Yes," he answered.

"You know, I was just there at Maidu's. She was thinking about leaving early since it was slow. Do you want me to call her to meet you here?"

"That would be great." A single cloud darkened the distant lake, but the sun was pleasantly warm on the shore. *Was there ever a best time for a confession?* Mark thought.

"I have a crazed man at the park, and he's about to be arrested unless a responsible party can guarantee his safety," Shannon said into the cellular phone. "He has identified you as the source of his delusions."

The ranger rested his booted foot on the bench, and on ending the call, advised Mark, "Buddy, there are no answers out there." Shannon spanned the view and then touched his chest over the heart. "They're all in here."

It had darkened when he heard the muted sound of rubber tires on gravel and the thud of a shut door. With the gentle steps leading to where they sat, Mark felt his life's worth.

"He just wanted to tan his penis," Shannon joked to

welcome Emilia. "Do you know this man?"

"You'll have to line him up with other naked men so I can be sure," she answered and took a seat next to Mark. "So, you've been raising hell out here?" She leaned to kiss him.

"I suppose it's safe to release him to your custody," the ranger said as he started toward the parking lot.

"But officer," Emilia interjected. "I am not going to be able to guarantee his safety for later tonight."

"As long as it's not in my jurisdiction," Shannon replied. "Have a good day."

Mark remained silent, holding her hand on his lap. He kissed her when she turned to begin a conversation. It was after a few deep breaths to clear his chest that he asked, "Will you go with me?"

"Anywhere you want," she replied and returned his gaze. "Where are we going?"

"Fort Hamilton, Nevada."

"What?" she blurted, and then returned her hands on his lap. "What's in Fort Hamilton?"

"I borrowed a life from an epitaph, and I want to return it," he answered without hesitation.

"I'm thinking Shannon was right—you are delusional!" she joked. "Isn't Hamilton a ghost town?"

"Yes, it is." He raised her hands from his lap. "I have my own life now, and I don't need a ghost trailing us."

"You're serious!" she exclaimed. "Why so somber, Mark? Is everything all right?"

He shivered when the breeze picked up strength and glanced to where the waves crashed louder onto the shore. "There's just not enough time." He looked away as if to an audience beyond her. "But when I'm with you, everything seems timeless."

"I suppose it's my turn to get lost in riddles. I don't

understand what you're talking about."

He looked at her face and touched the wrinkles of her puzzled stare. He stammered, "My doctor called this morning." *A truth left unsaid cannot exist,* he thought, *but is it then a lie?* "I don't know how to say it."

"Say what, Mark?"

"The doctor said I may have *a cute* form of leukemia and wants me to return to San Jose for more tests and treatment." He took a deep breath as if to end the discussion.

"Oh, Mark!" She reached for his hands and looked into his eyes. After a pause, she continued, "I'll go with you to San Jose. They gave me the week off. I can always extend it."

Mark looked away. "I hope you can understand," he said.

"Understand what?" Her voice was harsh as if to force out the emotions he had not revealed.

"I can't go through with any of it—the tests or the treatments," he answered and looked back at her. "The treatments are unlikely to succeed, so there's no reason for the tests."

"You have no options but to go," she said and took his hands with a firm grip. "I may only be a coffee shop waitress, but I know there are no 'cute forms of leukemia.' Without treatment, they are all killers… What if it's something that can easily be treated?"

Mark recalled the recent image of the black-hatted villain, knocked to a cloud of dust when the librarian swung open the glass door. If only words could wield such power.

Emilia abruptly turned away from him, and he lunged from his seat to kneel at her feet. With his hand on her chin, he reclaimed her stare. "Emilia, you have to understand why I can't go through with it."

"I can't allow you to die... without even trying." Her eyes filled with tears. "I can't deal with any more guilt."

"There's no guilt to be had." He wiped a tear that trickled down her cheek. "Emilia, with you I have a chance for a life I never considered having... Billy took his own life because he feared life without love... Until now, I've lived my life afraid to love for fear of being hurt. I can't go back—not when I have the chance of loving you."

He sat back onto his heels. "I survived by borrowing the life of a ghost. It was the life of a dead man—one who could never be vulnerable, whose life was fully narrated on a wooden tombstone. It simply read, 'Born April 7, 1891; died November 29, 1913.'

"He was only 22 years old, the same age I was then. Standing at the graveside, I began to imagine his life, in the setting of a goldmining town, more rewarding than mine... Eventually, I grew jealous."

"Why would you be jealous of a dead man?"

"Until then, I felt overwhelmed by guilt—that my father's death was God's punishment for my childhood pleas... I figured if I assumed the imagined dead man's life, I would live more carefree."

"What did he die of?" she asked.

"I don't know, but that didn't stop me from imaging a reason... As I stood over his grave, I actually heard the gun battle at the saloon where he sustained the fatal wound, as well as the cry of the chorus girl he had fought over." They both laughed. "He probably died of something less romantic, like consumption."

"What's that?"

"I think it's tuberculosis."

Emilia sat down on the sand next to him and

embraced him. "Before you were in my life," he said, "I was made of ink, but now my heart pumps the blood that gives me joy… I beg you to understand why I can't hide away in a twenty-percent chance of survival. To kill time in treatment and be away from you is to kill eternity… I'll take life on its own accord, even when the payoff is death."

Chapter 21

They strolled out of the park barefooted and, on nearing the gravel lot, Emilia suddenly turned and ran back. Into the momentum of her spin, Mark was whirled in her direction and watched her stop at the periphery of their conjoined imprints on the sand. She remained still, staring at the shadows. Abruptly, she lifted a foot and, with her toe, raked the sandy reflection of themselves. She returned to his side and smiled, "You didn't want ghosts trailing us."

"How will you manage with me?" he asked.

"I don't know," she replied, "but we'll soon find out." She wrapped her arm around his waist and led to their trucks.

◆◆◆

Mark had not wanted to sleep—not that night, or ever again. *If the wind blows*, he thought, *the dust will never settle.* But he could not hold his eyes open against all he had unraveled on that day. He was asleep before Emilia had prepared for bed.

In the morning, his first glance was to the wrinkled sheet at his side. He knew she had rested—the smell of her fragrance remained on the pillow he wrapped his arms around. From the footsteps above, he realized she was preparing breakfast in the kitchen.

"Have you ever fallen asleep while making love?" he asked from the doorway. He watched her scurry about the counter opposite to him.

"What?" She turned to him, her mouth half open in surprise.

"I've been admiring you for the last three minutes, and it dawned on me how much I still have to learn about you." His arms, at first folded at his chest, dropped to his sides.

Mark was late to dodge the egg thrown across the kitchen. "Oh, my god! I'm so sorry," she said. "I didn't mean to hit you. You were supposed to catch it. Oh, God, I'm so sorry!"

The yolk dripped from his forehead. "Not only do you have a good arm, but quite a temper." He wiped his brow and added, "But it only makes me want you more!"

"What?... Were you fooled by my sunny disposition?" She carried a dishtowel to where he stood. "I just wanted to make breakfast. Aren't you the man of habit who always has his eggs over and easy?" She cleaned the wall behind him and, with each swipe, her body swayed against his. "It can't get easier than this."

"Nor as pleasurable, and you did manage to get it all over me." He wrapped his arms around her from behind. "I'm thinking you also aim to fry the egg upon my own heat."

He kissed her, and she turned to him in his embrace. "Easy," she said softly with her lips on his. "Let me churn that fire." She untied the sash of his bathrobe.

"Breakfast has never been served like this." He let the bathrobe drop. "I want to love you with all my soul."

◆◆◆

"What about the country potatoes?" he asked on stepping out of the shower. "They're actually my favorite part of breakfast."

"Oh, I thought it would be me!" She rushed out of the bedroom, leaving Mark to dry under the heat lamp. "Come back upstairs when you're done."

Spiced with cilantro and bacon bits, the country potatoes were served with two eggs. "Delicious," he said and dipped buttered sourdough toast into the yolk. "Who would have thought—two fine breakfasts in one day!"

She stopped his hand from reaching for the napkin and leaned toward him. With a swipe of her tongue, she licked the breadcrumbs from his mustache and a bead of yolk on his lip.

"I can't wait 'til lunch," he said with his eyes closed as if to retain the pleasure. "It'll be my turn to cook. And be forewarned—revenge is sweet."

Emilia turned the scrambled egg on her plate. "Life was simple when I had all the answers."

"Don't tell me you don't." He sat back in his chair. "I was hoping to get them cheaply."

"At one time, I was comfortable making a judgement by how someone ate... For example, the sloppy yolk falling on your shirt." She let the fork drop to the plate and sat back on the chair. "But now, it seems I better second-guess everything I had considered."

"What are you saying? Do I make love without grace?"

"Don't get me wrong. It's almost poetry watching you enjoy breakfast, even when you never change the syntax." She shifted on her chair. "But I need to remember that no matter what we experience together, it'll only be a glimpse of who we are."

"To transcend *never* is what you're saying?" he asked.

She briskly stood up from her chair. "Come with me. I have some things to pick up from my house."

◆◆◆

The wind through the driver's window was all that stirred on the panorama of the lake. With only the sun seeming to have ambition, the lake appeared like an indigo glass fallen from the sky. At the lakeshore park, the snow had melted, yet the granite boulders continued their timeless march. Where the road rose above the shore, Mark stretched to see if, through the crystalline surface, he could gauge how deep the water was.

She turned into the wooded valley and drove among evergreens that rose tall from redwood stalks. Budding leaves were bountiful on the aspens and cottonwoods.

Distant in the meadow, two deer strolled among the grasses. It was springtime after a winter rest.

"It's all so beautiful, like a fairytale," Mark said. "You are Snow White, and I'll be her Happy dwarf."

"You've confused the fairytales again. It's Hansel and Gretel."

"You're right," he said, but added in a sober tone, "Is Hansel still over the fireplace mantle?"

"Of course," she answered and stopped the truck in front of the rock-faced cabin. "Come with me, little boy! I have some candies I'm sure you will enjoy'""

Unfettered in the warmth of spring, the wind chime pealed as he chased Emilia through the front door. In the living room, he reached for her from behind and said, "I don't need an oven to be fired up, or candy to be enticed. Touching you is enough to rouse my desire."

"Ooh!" she exclaimed and turned to him. "You are a poet and a bit of a cad!"

In his scan of the room, he saw that Bullwinkle's effigy was still on the mantle. "Oops!" he uttered, and then let his arms drop away from their embrace.

"What happened?" she asked.

"I'm sorry," he answered and feigned a chuckle. "I was spooked by your Bullwinkle friend."

"Hansel!" she corrected. "Isn't he the cutest? Maybe I should take him with me."

Mark turned away from the fireplace and walked to the bookcase on the opposite wall. He pretended to browse through a book of native art. "But what will you really be taking from your treasure chest?"

Without a word, Emilia walked past him into the bedroom. He snapped shut the book and waited for a summons. Bullwinkle's grin continued to taunt him. "Not this time!" Mark snarled in response.

"What did you say?" she called from the room.

"I... like your wind chime!" he replied.

"I got it from the Catskills," she said. "It keeps me alert to the spirits in the forest."

"That could be scary when you're here alone and in the dark." He watched her rummage through undergarments in the lower drawer of a bedside armoire.

She looked up to where he stood at the doorway. "Have a seat." She motioned to the bed. "There's no reason to be afraid of spirits. They exist everywhere... if we pay them attention."

He sat at the corner of the bed and dropped back on the mattress with an exaggerated bounce. Turned on his side, he watched as Emilia held up a bra. "Will you be modeling those?" he asked, but more earnestly added, "I would still be spooked, being here alone and thinking of ghosts."

"Like you were of Hansel?"

"Well, no. He just annoys me, but to know there are spirits of the dead watching me—that would scare me."

"I suppose it's just how one sees death." She sat on the side of the bed and let the negligee she had inspected drop to the floor. Mark rolled on the mattress and glanced up at the ceiling. Their silence was the confession of emotions concealed.

"I'll make sure no ghost trails us," she said with a conciliatory tone in her voice.

Mark remained silent: his death was not what he wanted to discuss. After a pause, he asked matter-of-factly, "Do you think Shakespeare lived passionately?"

"The questions you come up with!" she laughed. "Why would you want to know that?"

Reassured by her laughter, he reached for the bra she had set on the bed and spun it with his finger. "I need to know. It's important, because if great poetry comes from desire, more than from experiencing the pleasure, I'd better settle for writing you a mediocre poem."

She turned on the bed to lay next to him. "Your passion is poetry enough," she said and embraced him (*like the earth hugs the moon,* he thought).

Mark glanced at the framed photographs that hung on all walls. In the dim daylight, he focused his attention on them. "Emilia, why do you live alone?"

"I've been waiting for you."

"But I mean—" He wriggled out one arm from their embrace to point at the photo of her grandmother. "These are of your family. You seem to treasure their memories. Why aren't you with them, in Georgia or Oklahoma?"

"Where would we be then?" she replied.

As if propelled by a deep sigh, she sat up to the side of the bed and picked up a framed photograph from the night table. The yellow tint of aged paper and the gray light that sifted through the window made it difficult to discern the particulars of the characters.

He worked to focus on the black-and-white image of a young couple. "They seem much in love," he reckoned. "Are they your parents?"

She turned on the lamp behind the photograph. The soft light revealed the likeness of her in the couple. "Yes, it's a photo of my parents." She lay back on the bed but continued to stare at the photo. "They were young and very much in love," she said and rested the portrait on her chest. "It wasn't long after that picture was taken that their dreams were shattered."

Words are engendered with ideals, he recalled, *which we should live up to, in order to understand and affect our world.* But Mark felt impotent, unable to think of words to protect her from her apparent sorrow. He merely brushed his fingers through her hair.

"You talked of having borrowed a life from an epitaph," she began again, then gestured to the photos on the walls. "These have lent me a past... I suppose we both have ghosts to bury?"

"But these are real. They are of your family," he said. "They are who *you* are. You can't bury their memories."

"No... I can just carry them along with me... to glorify that one second of life these portray—in which everything was right. But there was much sorrow in their hearts, which they hid with smiles forever inscribed in those photographs. That is the ghost I've not yet come to terms with."

A riddle was a safe haven, he presumed, *in which to displace unsettled emotion*: an answer would be a shortcoming. He tightened their embrace... because it was all he could do.

Her voice trembled when she continued. "I didn't keep the newspaper clippings that reported *Indian woman kills self.*"

"I am so sorry!" he replied.

"So was I," she said and hesitated before adding, "But in being sorry, am I recognizing guilt?... and if there's a guilt, shouldn't there be punishment?"

"I didn't mean to—" Mark attempted a defense.

"What?" He had interrupted her deliberation, but she continued unaffected. "My grandmother, in her Christian way, would often tell me that there's no love where anger lingers, and it's only because of deepest love that anger can be sustained."

"Your grandmother is a wise woman, but is she referring to anger you carried?" he asked.

"Billy committed suicide and told no one why. I was devastated. And my father, who still called Billy 'the black boy from down the block,' told me he understood my sorrow and guilt." She paused. Her hands trembled, holding the frame to her chest. "He said that when my mother had driven the car off the road into the tree, she took his life along with hers. It was his guilt to be still alive... I had not known until then that she had committed suicide."

Mark wiped a tear from her eye.

"My father told me how since I was born, things had been difficult for my mother: she'd suffered bouts of hysteria and withdrawal."

Emilia returned the photo to the nightstand. "All I could say was *I'm sorry*... It's all I ever said to him about her death."

"So, with being sorry, you accepted guilt, not only for your mother's suicide but also Billy's. Was running away from your family the punishment?"

She rolled in bed to look at Mark. "I majored in psychology to find an answer, but there were none among the formulas and postulates— I decided then that science only allowed for man's arrogance. I then turned to religion, thinking it to be his humility; but in faith, I only found complacency." She laid her head on his chest. "And that's a very safe place in which to remain."

◆◆◆

Where Emilia had borrowed a past from the perpetual smiles on her family's photographs, he had buried his own, entrusting his passions onto the words he wrote. In her eyes, he saw no anger, only a desire for reconciliation. In himself was the absence of love, that now was joyfully blooming with Emilia.

She deserved unencumbered love, and he was committed to providing that. He promised to amend her sorrow and became mentally determined to retrieve his past.

Chapter 22

He touched his eyes to assure himself they were wide open: in the darkness of the room, he could not be certain. Scanning the visual void, he searched for a focus until suddenly a strip of light was cast to the foot of their bed. He followed it to the window above their heads and then beyond it to the forest that softened the radiance from the sun's glare. *Emilia's grandmother*, thought Mark, *would surely bless their sunrise union.*

Like Halloween phantoms, shadows in the room quickened in the flaring of the sunlight. Yet the chime remained silent: these could not be the spirits Emilia had talked about, but more likely his personal ghosts.

He slithered out of bed so as not to awaken her. At the door, he looked back and watched the gentle flicker of her closed eyelids. He hoped she was dreaming of him.

In the living room, the sunlight was still dim, so Mark followed a cool breeze to the fireplace. Even in the darkness, he noticed Hansel on the mantle. Discolored in shades of gray, the stuffed effigy sneered at him. With a fisted punch to the snout, Mark reformed its grin.

"I found the grace in love," he retorted, and then shadow-boxed a few more jabs. "Take that, Victor!" he added, pleased with Hansel's crimped grin.

Gradually, it became easier to maneuver about the room. On the bar table he found a binder packed with loose white paper. Like taking a sword from its scabbard, he pulled a pen out from the binder and firmly gripped it, as if to the hand of an old friend. *Ah, Shakespeare's passion*, he wondered, *were his words those of desire or tantric* (experiential divinity)?

"*The sword within the scabbard keep, and let mankind agree*," he recited from John Dryden. "I've chosen my weapon," he rebutted the quotation, "and it is passion… pressed from my heart and carried in my blood." Mark flailed the pen in the air and sat down to write. "And beware, sir, that into an ancient tomb it will not keep."

Words flowed from his hand, and ink bled from the pen. In the dim light, Mark felt every word she would read—it was the poem he had wanted for Emilia.

"What are you writing?" she asked from behind him. Mark jerked back in the stool, and the pen flew across the kitchen floor.

"Sorry. I didn't mean to scare you," she said.

"It's nothing." He leaned forward to shield the paper and folded it closed.

"You're acting awfully suspicious for it being nothing." She combed the back of his head with her fingers.

"It's just a poem." He swiveled the seat around to face her. "But you can't have it until I'm finished."

"You were serious about writing me a poem?"

With his arms wrapped around her waist, he replied, "Didn't you say my passion was poetry enough?"

"You are a quick learner."

"I hope so," he said.

"Oh, my god. What happened to Hansel?" Emilia's shriek pierced his ear.

He kept his stare away from the mantle. "Do you think my nose would grow if I told a lie? Let's see— it was an accident?" He continued to glare at the floor.

"Mark?" she chuckled. "I can't believe you're jealous of that hairball!"

"I'll fix it." He stood up and, at the mantle, straightened the Georgia Tech cap on its head. Hansel's snout could not be remolded. "It was an accident," he repeated but didn't turn to face her.

"Oh, give me a break!" she mocked exasperation. "Just go get dressed. I'll make us some coffee."

◆◆◆

Only lovers seem to do foolish things, Mark recalled Shannon comment on baring his chest to nap in the sun. Noticing her bra hanging from the lampshade and his torn clothes, he knew it was from last night's activities.

"You left me nothing to wear!" he shouted from the bedroom to Emilia in the kitchen.

"What do you mean?"

"You've torn everything I had to wear."

"I did no such thing," she said from the bedroom door. "Take a shower, and I'll get you something to wear."

"Not too much lace at the collar. It gives me a rash." He lowered his head to pass through the narrow doorway of the bathroom. "Wow!" he screamed under the spray of cold water from the shower head.

"Sorry, you have to let the water warm up for two minutes first," she called from the bedroom. "I left some things on the bed. I think they'll fit."

Water dripped from his hair when he stood to inspect the red flannel shirt and well-worn jeans Emilia had laid out at the foot of the bed. "Who owned these?

Johnny Appleseed or Paul Bunyan?" he asked. "They fit... perfectly!"

"Maybe not when you exhale." Emilia smiled from the door.

"You think they are tight?"

"A little more than when Victor wore them."

"Victor?" He dropped to the corner of the bed. "I thought the two of you were just friends."

"Jealousy is unbecoming of you," she said and started to fold his torn clothes. "Now don't go taking it out on Hansel."

"You did wash them?" His hands rubbed the thighs.

She sat next to him. "He left a few things with me when he moved to a smaller apartment. I think he meant to take those to Goodwill." In jest, she added, "Good thing, though. They've come in handy when I rip my men's clothes off."

At the table, she replaced the binder with a placemat, on which she set his breakfast.

"I thought you were just making coffee," he said.

"I felt guilty about your clothes," she said, placing a smaller plate for herself. "I hope you take this in compensation." She sat across from him and took a sip of the coffee. "I heard you awaken while it was still dark."

His eyes didn't waver from her glance. "I wanted to welcome the sunrise."

"I guess I must have fallen right back to sleep."

"It seemed like you were sound asleep when I thought I heard the wind chime."

Her hazel eyes shifted slightly from her focus. "But I know it didn't sound."

"It has been rather quiet. I suppose there's no wind."

"I put it away last night," she replied.

He grasped both her hands from across the table. "Will you go with me to Fort Hamilton?"

She pulled away from his hold and emptied the coffee into the sink. Glaring out the window, she replied. "I said I will go anywhere with you."

Mark embraced her from behind. "I have to do this," he said.

Chapter 23

US Highway 50 is designated as the loneliest road in America. With its well-deserved national recognition, the highway traverses mountains and desert basins in the heart of Nevada. Mark realized no other vehicle had come their way for more than forty minutes; and looking at the flat road ahead, none was soon anticipated.

The late morning sun seemed to glitter on the sagebrush, windblown across the desert basin. With the monotony of recurrent rents on the yellow median, his gaze became transfixed on the highway stripe that continued unbent ahead of them. With thoughts being his only distraction from the black asphalt, Mark reached, as if in reflex, to his shirt pocket for the note he recalled Sister Eugene had once pinned there; but instead of the note for his mother about his third-grade misbehavior, he felt the crinkle of the paper on which he had written a poem for Emilia.

He had completed the poem the previous morning, but her sullen face after committing to make the trip had kept him from editing it. He stowed it into the shirt pocket and attempted to enliven her resolve on going along with his journey.

In her kitchen, he had held Emilia while she

continued to stare out the window. "Let the guilt go," he had advised, but except for her grip on the sink, she remained impassive.

She was quick to pack for the week they would travel, but when he shut the door to her home, Mark felt that they had certainly left something behind. That night at his home, they shared childhood stories, but only to keep each other entertained.

"We don't have to go," he told her in bed.

"It's something you feel you have to do," she answered. "I'll get over it." Her breath in his ear was deep, her fingers on his chest were moist.

The phone rang at five in the morning, and she responded to the request to go into work. "They're short-staffed," Emilia explained and kissed him as she ran out of the darkened bedroom.

Garbage is what dinner becomes when it is not eaten, and when she arrived late from work, he told her the meal he had prepared was in hopes of retrieving her disheartened spirit.

"If I could surrender my guilt as casually as you have your life," she replied at the table, "I would have no hesitation to walk you to a sacrificial altar."

Tears are for sorrow, and solitude for despair, but he was unable to muster a response to what Emilia had said. He simply stared away.

She cleared the dishes and proposed to follow him to bed. Mark lay on the mattress and waited in the darkness, but it was hours before he heard the stairs creak on her footstep.

His back was turned, but from the hall light he saw Emilia's shadow entering the door. He kept his eyes closed in pretended sleep and heard her clothes drop at the foot of the bed. A draft lapped his skin when she lifted the comforter and a gale when she lay down next to him.

"Let's leave in the morning," she said.

◆◆◆

A guitar carried the tune of a train on a track, and a harmonica was at the whistle. "Let's make this a night we'll never forget," Emilia sang along with Suzy Boggus on the radio. "There's time for one more; one more for the road."

In the middle of the Nevada Great Basin, the only station they were able to tune into was country-western. *Just as well*, Mark thought, as Emilia's mood appeared to have recovered.

While directing the truck on the relentless straight highway, he would glance at Emilia, singing with her eyes shut as if the journey she sang about was her own. Her hair streamed through the slit of the window and was tousled by the wind outside the truck. He tapped his fingers on the steering wheel, in rhythm with the music.

They had started out early that morning, but he felt as if he had not slept at all. While they had packed, Emilia remained quiet, which he hoped was from weariness and not a change of mind.

"We should take my camping gear," she said, with it already at hand. "It's pretty comfortable for two people."

There was not much room left in the back of the truck when he loaded what she thought they might need. He joked a woman always made for a resourceful traveling companion, for there was nothing they would lack. That is until it had to be carried—she seemed not to hear.

She sat on the front passenger seat with the map

opened on her lap. "Maybe we can have breakfast outside Carson," she suggested, but it was not until Silver Springs that they stopped. He needed coffee to keep his eyes open.

"I think we'll make good time," she said after the waitress took their order.

Mark remembered the Harley Davidson couple at Topaz Lake, who traveled on schedule toward Las Vegas. Their love, tattooed on their arms, survived even their cruel banter. Why, Mark thought, would he feel threatened by Emilia's silence at the table?

"We're not on our way to a funeral," he answered his own thought aloud. "I only meant it metaphorically."

A drop of condensation trickled down the side of her glass.

"What?" she asked, appearing confused.

"Returning to the ghost town... Reclaiming my life."

"And under what pretense," she replied, "do you reclaim a life by relinquishing it to a challenge?"

He strained in her glance and replied. "Leukemia is more than a challenge... It is, in fact, the consumption of a life."

"You're being melodramatic. You don't even know if that's what you have." She rested back in the chair.

"What I do have is what you have given me." He folded his hands and leaned forward to the table. "The pleasure of being a man. The joy of your love and of loving you. That... I don't want to put on hold, nor compromise. That's what I've done throughout my life."

"Remember what you said about why Billy killed himself?" she asked. "That he was afraid of living without love. Well, there are consequences for loving; but more importantly, there is a responsibility to sustain that love... All I want is for you to realize your responsibility in seeking this metaphor that sidetracked you."

To confront guilt, one needed to understand the accusation, but that had eluded him: for he had been a child, influenced by magical thought and scripture. His father's death was not a result of mystical wishes, but it did become a convenient displacement for a fear that inadvertently had engrossed his life.

Love he once thought would provide a resolution; but what Emilia proposed was that his own absolution was not in love, but in his will to sustain it—then, to endure the consequence.

◆ ◆ ◆

Blue, steel cold pierced the distance... and he recognized the features that were of leukemia. Mark cringed at the subconscious association with the clear sky ahead.

"Given more time to laugh and dance"
—Emilia sang along with Vince Gill—
"Given more time to have the chance,
To show you this is where I want to be
Lord, I wish I was given more time—
For you and me."

She returned Mark's gaze, and Vince continued on the radio, solo.

"I love it when you smile," he said, and reached for the hand she placed on his lap.

Emilia slid toward the middle of the seat and rested her head on his shoulder. She stared at the distant range. "Getting tired?"

"A little, but I don't think we have much more to go."

In the rear-view mirror, he noticed mushroom clouds rise above the crest of the mountain ranges and threaten to rain. Ahead of them was the perennial thirst he used to describe the lackluster desert. Other than the shadows from the heavens, the colors of the panorama never seemed to vary. Only tan rocks on sandy soil, cropped by sagebrush, appeared to reflect the radiance from the sun.

"Do you think it'll rain?" he asked.

"The weather report has it to be clear and dry, at least through tomorrow," she answered.

"Let's hope those clouds following us aren't going to drop their load on our campsite. I want to be able to count the stars while we share a sleeping bag."

"That sounds nice," she replied, "and we'll also be able to get up together for the sunrise."

An adventure involved not knowing but only anticipating. Looking back at the darkening sky behind them, Mark considered a recourse for the worse case it would rain. *We pattern our lives for comfort when we are most afraid of its challenges*, he recalled Emilia elaborating on himself as a man of habit. *Under what pretense do you reclaim a life by relinquishing it to a challenge?*

"I thought they would have paved it by now," he said about the turnoff gravel road from US 50. "I hope it's not like this the entire way to Hamilton."

"How long ago was it since you were here last?" She sat back into the seat. "It looks kind of rough."

A lifetime, he thought to say, but answered, "Twenty years."

"Maybe we should set up camp first." She pointed to a campground and the *No Services* sign at the entrance to Humboldt National Forest.

"I'd just as well go on before it gets dark."

Dry rivulets furrowed across the road to form deep clefts on the decline of the hill. Granite boulders appeared to hold sentry at each turn, and the sagebrush of the basin yielded to pine at the higher altitudes.

"Thank God for four-wheel drive," he said. "I suppose they haven't gotten around to repairing the road since winter."

Emilia looked at the mountain ahead of them. "There's still quite a bit of snow at the top. You think we should go on?"

"It looks like it's only above the tree line. Hamilton should be well below that."

◆ ◆ ◆

The road became level at the timberline, and in a clearing of the forest was a small wooden shelter. A mound of snow lingered in the shade of its ramshackle porch. Mark pulled at the locked bolt on the wooden door and read the sign: it required tourists to deposit a five-dollar park entry fee into an adjacent secure box.

"From the look of the place, I don't imagine a ranger will be by in the near future," Emilia called out to him from her seat in the truck.

"Well, then, we'll save the five dollars." He slipped the bill back into the pocket of his jeans.

Driving on into a valley, the skeleton foundations of Hamilton were less than a mile from the station. In the shadow of *Treasure Hill*, the ruins reminded Mark of the trough of shattered dreams he enjoyed writing about, but now realized his was among them. He stopped the truck at two weathered brick posts, vestiges of the courthouse.

"There's not much left," she said as she stretched outside the truck.

"There never was," he replied. Turning around from the brick posts, he added, "There were only illusions… for which so many lives were spent."

A sudden gust of wind tumbled sagebrush away from their feet and stole the hollow sound of the truck doors closing. Vacant brick stairs, molded by the step of wind and water, channeled the trail they followed. Wooden studs without walls, like a forest after a fire, rose from the ground. Shrubs reclaimed concrete slabs. They walked along Main Street.

"Are we fools to be led by dreams?" he asked.

"Are we fools to do otherwise?" she answered.

Prosperity had bypassed most of the townspeople by the time of their death. Instead of marble, the headstone they read at the entrance to the cemetery was hand carved on granite rock. Its inscription was a farewell to a beloved wife, dead at childbirth. It stood alone.

"Do you think the child lived on?" Emilia asked.

"Epitaphs are unfair. They only tease our curiosity, and entice imaginations like mine to fantasize about the untold story." He walked through the brush and glanced at every tombstone. "No wonder I was *sidetracked*... But now, I can't even remember where it was."

Most of the epitaphs were difficult to read. Rain and snow had withered the wood on which many had been written, and windborne gravel had pelted the inscriptions. At the outskirts of the cemetery, hidden in foliage, partly buried by soil, Mark found the wooden marker for which he searched.

"*Died 1873*," he read aloud. "It once read *Mark, age 22*, but this has to be the one."

Mark stood still, his gaze fixed to the earth. Emilia knelt and cleared the space of brush with her hands.

"He should be in there," he said and stared at the area where he'd imagined a burial mound. In his introspection, he tried to recall the fantasy that once had been inspired, and wondered why the inscribed eulogy that didn't even merit a sentence would have provoked his envy. After all, it was only dirt and stone under the soles of his feet.

"There never was a life to borrow," he solemnly declared. "It was only an excuse."

A golden band striped the cherry-rose fluffs of clouds that drifted over the western ridges. The mustard-colored sage Emilia had cleared tumbled with a breeze toward the town below the cemetery. Mark knelt where she had stopped to listen.

"It's been easier to blame what I could not control than to gamble and endure the consequences." He held her hands. "If to die is to be without you, I will endure whatever it be to live forever."

"Let's go on to San Jose," she said and led him back to the truck.

◆◆◆

The clouds that had threatened them from the rear-view mirror now cast an early nightfall from above them. Mark glanced at the dashboard clock to assure it was not as late as he presumed from the darkness.

Emilia strapped her seat belt on. "I guess we won't be able to see the stars tonight."

"We might as well head back. Eureka is about a three-hour drive. We could spend the night in a motel." He felt the chill of damp air when he settled into the driver's seat. "It's probably going to rain."

"So much for weather reports," she added. "I just hope it doesn't snow. It would be rough on that road out of here."

On their return, the ranger station was not as distinct

in the darkness, appearing as if an outcropping from the forest; but shortly after they passed it, the rain began to fall.

Sounding like pellets on the truck's metal, sheets of water curtained the windshield. At intervals, the wiper swiped at his visual field, and Mark struggled to keep a steady focus on the dimly-illuminated road descending the mountain.

Flashes of lightning were reflected on the walls of granite and silhouetted the forest on either side of the hill. Water filled the rivulets, and the truck tires gripped the gravel with four-wheel traction. He felt confident for their safety.

With the crash of thunder and a reflected flash of lightning, a boulder smashed into the front of the truck. Mark struggled to control the spin of the steering wheel.

As the truck rolled, the windshield burst into shattered glass, and the metal frame crumbled. When the dashboard was jammed into his left flank, he released the seatbelt and turned to shield Emilia. His pain was disregarded for fear that she would be hurt.

Metal scraped against rock on every roll of the truck. Mud oozed through the dented doors, as shrubs slapped at either side. The din inside their chamber seemed to cast its own dimension, and the unremitting rattle suspended time.

Silence erupted as if the world had ended. He sat still and held Emilia tight. Counting the drops of rain that sounded on the ceiling, he knew the storm had passed. A brief spill of gravel disrupted the quiet, and he expected their tumble to resume. But the truck remained lodged against the bark of a tree.

Fate grants no terms and accepts no bargains, he thought, but the courage he awaited was granted when he felt her stir in his arms.

"Are you all right?" Emilia asked.

Mark pulled away from the dashboard that pressed against his side. Pain surged from his flank on the turn. He held back the scream swelling within his lungs and remained motionless, waiting for the pain to subside.

"Mark, are you okay?"

"Yes," he said and noticed her touch dripped with moisture that smelled of blood. He fastened his glance towards her voice, but only the gloss of her hair was apparent in the dark. "Oh, God, are you all right?"

"Yes, I'm okay. How did it happen?"

"I think we were hit by a rock-slide." He looked ahead through the soiled slime that screened the broken windshield. A single beam from a headlight illuminated a mound of rock and mud, in which the truck was partly buried. A thin cropping of trees stood on a forty-five-degree incline.

"Can you tell how far from the road we've fallen?" she asked. Her side window was intact but was covered under a heap of debris. "At least we've landed right-side up."

The driver's door was caved in and jammed against a tree. There was only blackness everywhere he turned. The inside lamp worked.

"Mark," she said. "There's blood on your chest."

Deep abrasions on his left side oozed blood. It hurt when he raised his arm to lift the shirt. "It looks like only scrapes," he assured her.

"I have a first-aid kit." She motioned toward the disarray of their gear and added, "Somewhere back there."

The luggage was strewn onto the downhill side of the truck, but a clearing led to the rear door, which had burst open.

"Let's get some of this stuff out, and I can get you bandaged up." She climbed over the seat and out the rear door.

"Ohhh!" he moaned when he made the effort to climb out.

"Mark, are you sure you're all right?" Emilia returned with a towel. "Here, hold this against the cuts while I look for the kit."

He pressed the towel against the wounds and watched the blood seep through to drip between his fingers: *Kind of thin, ain't it?* he recalled the nurse's observation.

"I think I broke a rib." He felt pain with the pressure of his hand.

Emilia returned and applied a bulky dressing. "Sit up," she said and wound an Ace wrap around his chest, applying pressure at the wounds.

"Have you got a silver bullet?" he asked through gritted teeth. "Didn't it all begin like this—you nursing me?"

"No, it all began with a bit of yolk on your lip."

She stared at the bandage she had wrapped and waited to assess for seepage of blood. Without the hazel tint noticeable, her eyes seemed solemn, not with the cheer he recalled when she first glanced at him over the corrugated edges of a newspaper at the café counter.

"I think the bandage will hold. I don't see fresh bleeding." Emilia carried the kit to the backpack she had left outside and returned with his down jacket. "It's pretty cold outside. You better put this on."

His side hurt when he moved the arms, but he managed to get the jacket on. Emilia helped him climb over the seat and out through the back of the truck.

"It's a bit of a hike up to the road," she said. "You go on up. I'll put everything we need into one pack and carry it with me."

"I can carry it," he said, but he buckled with pain when reaching for it. "All right, so I won't." He carried the two sleeping bags instead.

The altitude had never before challenged him as much as the fatigue he felt while climbing up to the road. He sat on a fallen rock and panted to catch his breath.

"Mark, what's the matter?" she asked and let drop the backpack. She knelt in front of him and looked at his face. "You're so pale... It's got to be more than a broken rib."

He could not reply and only wished they were in bed, with the softness of her flesh next to him.

She unzipped his jacket and raised the shirt. The bandage was still dry. "I'll set up the tent here and then walk to the highway to get some help. You get some rest."

"No!" He did not mean to shout, but he was afraid it would not have come out.

Tears flowed from her eyes. "You need help. I've got to get you to a doctor." Emilia walked to the pack.

Wolves don't howl to the sunrise, he thought looking up to the thick canopy of trees. There would not be much to see of the sky from where they were. The ranger station was at the edge of the forest and faced east. It was a much better place, he thought, to set up camp.

"We're less than a mile from the ranger station," he strained to say. "It'll take you a day to walk to the highway."

"But we need to get you to a hospital."

"A ranger will come before you can even reach the highway." He stood up slowly, with the sleeping bags held to brace his chest, and walked toward Hamilton. "The ranger will stop at the station."

The drag of his step on the gravel sounded an iambic rhythm and reminded Mark of his poem. "There's no greater overture of love than through poetry," he repeated for Emilia but was not able to recite the poem in his pocket.

"The chestnut grows best where the tree blooms fall," she said at his side.

"Passion flourishes nearest from whence it came—you and me," he replied.

◆◆◆

A mist appeared suspended over the chaparral in the valley at the end of the uphill road. That they had seen the ranger's cabin in daylight allowed them to find it in the moonless night. Mark rested on the porch.

"There may be a phone inside." Her attempt to pry open the door with a knife failed; but the door burst open when she heaved her shoulder against it. "Pretty damn good for a student of religious studies, wouldn't you say?"

Even in the dark, the cloud of dust discharged inside was reflected by the scant light from outside. She waited for the particles to settle and then began to search the cabin.

"Come inside. It feels a little warmer," she called out to Mark. Just to the side of the door, she found a lantern. The kerosene within the copper reservoir sloshed when she lifted it. "Good thing I brought some matches."

She set the wick to burn dimly, in hopes of making it last throughout the night. With the lantern placed on a nightstand, she centered it in the room. A small desk rested at the opposite end to the door. With her finger, she brushed a layer of dust on the flat top. "I don't think anyone has been here for a long while," she quietly said to herself.

Inside a steel file cabinet, she found only the droppings of rodents. Against the sidewall was a cot with most of its springs broken off, and a haggard mattress that sagged through them. At a back corner was a cast-iron wood burner, but its chimney pipe lacked a segment to the roof. Nothing in the room, she determined, was twentieth century.

She dusted off the mattress and turned to the front of the room.

Mark slowly entered and slouched onto a wooden chair.

"I'll roll out the mattress on the floor," she said, a tear streaking a trail on her soot-covered cheek. "It should be more comfortable than just the sleeping bags."

"You've been crying," he said and attempted to touch her.

She had set the mattress out on the porch and sat at his feet. Rubbing his hands to relieve their cold, she glanced up and noticed him struggle to keep his eyes open.

He saw her quickly look away and felt the grip of her hand tighten. "You are beautiful," he said but felt his lips lose the smile to a shiver. "I did come further than half a tank of gas… didn't I?"

"Why are you talking like this?" She straightened to lie next to him. "Get some rest." She kissed him on the lips. "The ranger should be here in the morning."

He licked for her taste on his lips. "There's always a beautiful sunrise after a storm," he said and looked up at the black sky on which only stars sparkled. "I'm hoping your mother will tell you she approved of me."

◆ ◆ ◆

He felt a cold breeze fan his face. She had ensured the rest of him was covered inside their sleeping bag and embraced him firmly to the warmth of her flesh. A dim flicker of light from the lantern appeared to dance on the ceiling as he turned his gaze to far beyond the platform of the porch. Sagebrush tumbled across the valley, and Mark watched Emilia pull her arm from under their cover to reach out among a billion stars; her finger then dipped into the celestial void.

Embraced with Emilia, he kept a watch for the last star on the horizon.

Biography

Carlos Alvarado grew up in California and now lives in Florida. *Cry WaterColors* is his first book. The present *d2-Edition* is a 2019 look back on his writing. Recently, he published a second novel, *Tujunga*, a thrilling conspiracy that is romantically told. Mr. Alvarado is a retired Emergency Medicine physician. Contact the author at www.calvarado.me

Background Notes:

1.   The prologue is somber in character and transcendental in imagery, but it was best for illustrating the depth of Mark's childhood religious confusion that became his silent torment. This introduction to Mark's state of mind explains why his psyche would forever be affected upon the death of his father, and why he would continue into adulthood a lifestyle that was self-destructive.

2.   Significant change in our behavior rarely occurs out of simple desire, but is more likely incited by a painful event. In Chapter 1, that turning point occurs for Mark: where from the depth of his desperation and in the silence of a prostitute, he recognizes the searing pain of his loneliness. Inspired to amend self-protective mechanisms developed from childhood, he sets out to reclaim his emotional life.

3.   The concept of *tantric sex* was introduced by an entrepreneurial woman Mark encountered at the gym. But in fact, it was the enlightenment of such a relationship he aspired for, and was developing with Emilia.

4.   In coming of age, we learn much about ourselves from those with whom we come in contact. In this book, there are a number of characters, such as Trapper Garza, that offered Mark an emotional mirror (much as the *Spirit of Christmas Past* did for Ebenezer Scrooge).

5.   I am always amazed how picayune traits can cause significant reactions from other individuals. In Mark's case, it was the egg-yolk that often stained his lips on eating breakfast which piqued Emilia's unrelenting curiosity. As a free spirit searching for truth from wherever it would come, Emilia was drawn to follow the simple to its complicated core.

6.   *Mutualism* is a relationship based on the appreciation of complimentary traits, as would be required in Tantra. As pointed out by Emilia, and recognized by Mark, these traits are often the physical and emotional differences between lovers that enhances their attraction.

7.   A major self-imposed challenge was Mark's quest to discern what Emilia meant with *Love without grace*: "Victor is a wonderful man, but he hides his emotional shortcomings in his physical attributes. With him, there's nothing a good fuck will not heal."

8.   Intermittent weakness Mark experienced, such as in the market, was a writer's literary freedom to exaggerate the symptom of anemia, which is what Leukemia often leads to. The anemia was further suggested by the nurse commenting on his blood--"kind of thin." Mark also recalled this when he noticed his blood after the accident.

9.   Leukemia is an insidious disease that often times results in an enlarged spleen. Located on the left flank/upper abdomen, the spleen is protected from common injury by the overlying lower ribs of the chest wall. When enlarged (such as because of leukemia) the spleen is more vulnerable to traumatic injury as it extends below the naturally protective bony cage. During the accident, Mark received major impact to his left flank from the driver-side door. Such trauma can result in a major rupture of the spleen and a sudden fatal hemorrhage; or a minor tear can lead to a slow bleed that would require surgical intervention to prevent death. In Mark's case, there would not be an opportunity for resuscitation.

10.   Mark mentioned how travelling with a woman would make the trip more comfortable by the fact *they* tend to pack all that would be required. That Emilia had packed the eventually much necessary first-aid kid showed her resourcefulness. There would be no need to fret on her ability to seek help when deep in the wilderness.

11.   In Chapter 1, Mark mentioned how words can affect our reality and later writes a paragraph that irks him for its melodrama. Yet, he succumbs to the tale the paragraph described and waits for the last star in the horizon on sunrise, as had Sadie to greet the spirit of her dead father.